PRAISE FOR THAT MAN 5

"With *THAT MAN 5*, Nelle L'Amour proves she's the Queen of Sexy Romantic Comedy. Blake Burns will once again make you laugh, cry, and swoon."

—Arianne Richmonde, USA Bestselling Author of The Star Trilogy

"Holy mother of a finale! *THAT MAN 5* just filled my heart with pure joy and happiness. And the writing, the one-liners, the hot crazy sex…I cannot even begin to articulate what an amazing storyteller Nelle is, and I'm in awe of her ability to have made this series get better and better, hotter and hotter with each book."

—A is for Alpha, B is for Books Blog

"Way worth more than 5-stars. A MUST READ!!! So right up there with the *Stark* series and the *Beautiful Bastard* series."

—Johnnie-Marie Howard, Reviewer

"Author Nelle L'Amour is on top of her game. Right up there with Emma Chase and Christina Lauren. There's no funnier, sexier, or more original book boyfriend than Blake Burns."

—Adriane Leigh, USA Today Bestselling Author of Beautiful Burn

"*THAT MAN* has it all—love, drama, mystery, craziness, heartbreak, sweetness and lots and lots of scorching sex scenes that made me a hot me a hot mess. Bravo, Ms. L'Amour, for such an amazing, beautiful love story!"

—Give Me Books

"WOW! Let me tell you you're in for a thrill ride. This series is in my Top 5. You won't be able to get enough of Blake and his tiger!"

—Summer's Book Blog

"A perfect way to end the series. Be prepared to cry, throw things and swoon over Blake once again."

—Book Avenue Reviews

"An emotional rollercoaster. A kickbutt hero. It's been an absolutely amazing journey witnessing Blake and Jen's love flourish."

—Fairest of All Reviews

"A sweet, crazy, and dynamic love story. One I soon won't forget."

—Love Betweeen the Sheets

"An awesome end to a fantabulous series. This is one series that will definitely stay in my hoard of books."

—My Book Filled Life

"Flove this series! Nelle warned us to 'Be prepared to laugh, cry, and swoon.' Boy did I!!!"

—Chasing Orion's Rouge Odyssey

"I experienced every emotion possible reading this last installment. Jennifer and Blake's passion and energy make for unforgettable scenes. As Blake's Grandma always says: *Zei gezunt.* Enjoy!"

—As You Like It Reviews

BOOKS BY NELLE L'AMOUR

Seduced by the Park Avenue Billionaire

Strangers on a Train (Part 1)
Derailed (Part 2)
Final Destination (Part 3)
Seduced by the Park Avenue Billionaire (Box Set)

An Erotic Love Story

Undying Love (Book 1)

Gloria

Gloria's Secret (Book 1)
Gloria's Revenge (Book 2)
Gloria's Forever (Book 2.5)

That Man Series

THAT MAN 1
THAT MAN 2
THAT MAN 3
THAT MAN 4
THAT MAN 5

THAT MAN 5

THAT
MAN
5

NELLE L'AMOUR

Nelle L'Amour thanks you for your understanding and support. To join her mailing list for new releases, please sign up here: http://eepurl.com/N3AXb

NICHOLS CANYON PRESS
Los Angeles, CA USA

THAT MAN 5
By Nelle L'Amour

Cover by Arijana Karcic, Cover It! Designs
Proofreading by Karen Lawson
Formatting by BB eBooks

To THAT MAN…Blake Burns

I will miss you.

And to all of you who fell in love with him.

THAT MAN 5

Chapter 1

Blake

Speeding back to my office, my pulse was in overdrive. My unexpected encounter with Kat at Saks had unhinged me. The fucking bitch!

My nerves were buzzing. I couldn't trust her. Not one bit. I hadn't yet told Jennifer a thing. The timing sucked. Fatigued and frazzled by her heavy period, the pressures of work, and all the wedding craziness, she just didn't need to hear something that might send her over the edge. In retrospect, I should have told her a long time ago. What had happened wasn't really my fault, but it was something I wasn't proud of. I wanted to forget. Keep the memory buried.

Should I tell her now? Fuck. I had to. Before she heard it from that sick bitch, who I knew would twist the story and make me look like a total shit.

At the first red light on Wilshire Boulevard, I reached into my pants pocket for my cell phone. Balls. It wasn't there. It must have fallen out in the dressing room at Saks. I made a sharp U-turn and headed straight back to the store. My heart was racing. I'd given Kat plenty of lead time.

Foregoing the slow elevator, I bounded up the emergency stairs to the third floor, taking two steps at a time. Working out weekly at the steep Santa Monica Stairs had its benefits.

"Looking for this?" my personal dresser Daniel asked as I exited the stairwell. My phone was in his hand.

I was breathing hard, not because I was winded, but because I was stressing.

I huffed a loud breath of relief as he handed me the phone. "Thanks, man," I said and then hurried to the elevator. Before I could speed-dial Jen's number, the phone rang. I glanced down at the caller ID screen and hit answer. It was Mrs. Cho.

"Mr. Burns, Jennifer call me. She say to tell you she going home."

"What do you mean?" My heart was hammering.

"She cry on phone. She say something bad happen."

God fucking damn it. I was too late. Kat had gotten to her.

I repeatedly pounded the down button but with no results. Fucking worthless piece of shit. Impatient, I flew back down the emergency stairs.

Fifteen minutes later, I pulled up to my condo building, relieved I hadn't gotten a speeding ticket. Leaving my car with the valet, I raced up to my apartment.

Silence.

"Jen! Jen? Are you here?" Frantically, I dashed from room to room, calling out her name. Fuck. Where was she?

I phoned her again. Her cell went straight to voicemail. I left her an urgent message, telling her to call me back right away. A chill skittered down my spine. Maybe, she'd never want to talk to or see me again. Once again, I'd deceived her.

Impulsively, I called my sister at her office. Perhaps, she knew something.

"Hi, Blake. What's up?" Her voice sounded unusually warm and friendly.

"Marcy, while she was there, did Jennifer get a call or text that upset her?"

"No. We had a lovely lunch, and then I believe she was heading back to her office. What's going on?"

Rushing my words, I told her what I believed had happened. My sister was one of the few people who knew what had gone down between Kat and me. Kat's file was sealed in her office.

"Jeez, Blake. Why didn't you tell Jen?"

"I don't know. I should have. But I didn't." *Stupid me.*

"Blake, it wasn't all your fault." Marcy's voice was softer and compassionate.

"I know. But I'm sure crazy Kat twisted things. With all her trust issues, Jen probably believed her. She didn't go back to the office."

"Shit. Blake, you've got to find her and explain what happened before everything blows up again."

Pacing my bedroom, I blew out a heavy breath of air. "My secretary said she was going home, but she's not here." My heart beat into a frenzy. Maybe the news had upset her so much she got into a car accident. She was after all Calamity Jen. But then I calmed down. For sure, I'd know that by now. "Marcy, what should I do?"

"Try calling her again, and then try one of her friends. Maybe they know something."

Marcy was always the smart one. Made sense. After trying Jen one more time, I'd try Libby.

I thanked my sister and told her not to say anything to our parents...at least not yet.

She assured me she wouldn't. "Good luck, Blake. And call me the minute you hear from her." She paused. "Love you, lil' bro."

Her unexpected affectionate words touched me, and I thanked her again. I quickly ended the call and speed-dialed Jen one more time. Shit. Nada. Wasting no time, I scrolled through my contacts and hit Libby's name. Fortunately, Jennifer had given me her number in case of an emergency. This was an emergency. Jen was leaving me.

Libby's phone, like Jen's, went straight to voicemail. Damn it. She was probably in a focus group or traveling. In a state of panic, I redialed Mrs. Cho. Perhaps she knew more. And had heard from Jen.

"Mrs. Cho, you said Jennifer went home, but she's not at my condo."

"No, no, Mr. Burns. She go home to her mother. She say big emergency."

Jesus. It was worse than I thought. Yup. A big emergency. I'd broken her heart.

"Cancel all my meetings and get Travel to book me on the next available flight to Boise."

Quickly, I changed from my suit into a pair of jeans, a T-shirt, and my leather bomber jacket. I retrieved my overnight bag from my closet and hastily threw in a hodgepodge of cool-weather clothes and bare necessities.

One hour later, I was on Delta Flight 4820, heading non-stop to Boise. I was comfortably seated in first class. But my heart was painfully seated in my throat.

Chapter 2

Jennifer

I immediately spotted my mother sitting in the waiting room of St. Luke's and sprinted up to her. The minute I'd heard the news, I'd headed straight to LAX, running a red light and narrowly missing a head-on collision. I didn't even go home to pack a bag. I needed to get to Boise as fast as possible and could always borrow some of my mom's clothes. My heart hadn't stopped galloping.

"Mom!"

My mother sprung from her chair at the sound of my voice. Her eyes were swollen red, and tears were swimming down her face. We exchanged a hug.

"Oh, honey, I'm so glad you're here," she sniffed.

"How's Dad?"

She dabbed at her tears with the dainty lace-trimmed hankie she was holding. Her lips quivered. "I don't know yet. He's still in surgery."

A horrific, freak thing had happened. While he was taking an afternoon stroll through our neighborhood, a car had hit him. The driver's brakes had given out, and he'd lost control. The car had swerved off the road, pinning my father against a telephone pole.

"The driver feels so bad. He wanted to stay until Dad got out of surgery, but I told him to go home to his family."

I squeezed my mom's free hand. That was so like her. To be forgiving, no matter what the circumstances. Deep inside, I hoped this virtue had been passed on to me. I encouraged her to sit down and took the vacant seat next to hers.

"Honey, does Blake know what's going on?"

"I tried to call him, but haven't been able to reach him." As much as he depended on it, Blake was forever forgetting, misplacing, or losing his cell phone. Retrieving my phone from my shoulder bag, I tried him one more time. No answer. Straight to voicemail. Instead of leaving a message, I hung up and texted him.

In Boise. Desperately need to talk to u.

In my anxious state, I inadvertently hit send before adding my customary *"xo."* And then my cell phone died. Without my charger, I now wouldn't know if he received my text or was trying to reach me.

I held my mom's hand as we waited patiently for news. My stomach was in knots. The minutes crawled by like hours, and from time to time, I could hear her soft sobs.

"Oh, honey, I'm so scared. What if—"

I cut her off. "Mom, he's going to be okay. I know it." I squeezed her icy hand, trying hard to believe my own words.

At close to six, a doctor met us in the waiting room. He introduced himself—Dr. Kumar. His accented voice was soft and melodic and suggested he was likely from India. He was wearing scrubs and a surgical mask atop his head. With his boyish good looks, the handsome physician looked too young to be an accomplished surgeon, but I reminded myself that St. Luke's was the best hospital in Boise and was, in fact, one of the top surgical hospitals in the country. I'd been here once when I'd gotten my tonsils out as a child.

My mom jumped to her feet and met his gaze. "Is my husband all right?" Her voice was small and shaky, and her eyes were still watering.

The brown-skinned doctor pressed his lips thin and swiped sweat off his forehead. "He's in critical condition."

"What does that mean, doctor?" I asked before my trembling mother could say a word.

"He sustained a head injury. We did an MRI and there's brain swelling. We won't know until tomorrow if he has sustained permanent damage."

His words were like a knife to my heart. The thought of my dad the professor not having his faculties was unbearable. Like my mother, I was an alarmist, but

I had to be brave for her.

"Oh dear Lord," she muttered. Her hand flew to her mouth, and a new torrent of tears poured down her cheeks. All air left my lungs as tears rushed to my eyes too. Afraid my mother might faint, I wrapped my arm around her frail shoulders as the doctor continued.

"He also sustained multiple fractures to his right leg. We did a bone graft and set it with pins."

Words were trapped in my weeping mom's throat. Holding it together as I best as I could, I asked the doctor if we could see him. The only good news, if you could call it that, was we could.

They had transported my dad from recovery to a small room in the intensive care unit. Still unconscious, he was hooked up to a myriad of bleeping monitors and IV bags, and an oxygen mask covered his face. His breathing was labored. A wide bandage swathed his head, and beneath the fabric of his blanket, I could see the outline of a thick toe-to-thigh cast.

"Oh, Daddy!" I cried silently. Tears stung the back of my eyes, and a painful lump filled my throat. I wasn't prepared for seeing him like this. So lifeless and vulnerable. All my life, my handsome, brilliant dad had always been strong and there for me. He almost never got sick. And now this. There were no Scrabble words in the world to describe the tangle of emotions that ate away at my heart. Sobs clogged my throat, but I held them back to be a pillar of strength for my mom.

"Oh Harold, darling," she choked, gently running her fingertips along his slack jaw. "Can you hear me? I love you so much. So very much."

My father stirred just a bit as if he'd heard her. At that moment, I was overwhelmed by the love my parents shared. A love so pure, so deep, so everlasting. A love for richer and poorer. In sickness and in health. I thought about Blake. And wondered—would this be us?

A sweet voice intercepted my thoughts. A nurse. She told us visiting hours were over.

My mother dabbed her tears with her soaked hanky and searched the nurse's kind, dark eyes. "Please can I stay? I want to be here for him when he wakes up."

If he wakes up.

A warm smile flickered on the nurse's face. "I don't see why not. I'll order a cot."

"Mom, I want to stay too."

The nurse responded. "I'm afraid, dear, we can allow only one person to stay in the room. Hospital regulations."

Disappointed, I cupped my mother's shoulders. "Are you going to be okay, Mom?"

She nodded. "I'll call you, honey, if there's any change."

For the better, I prayed silently. I hugged her good night. Then, lightly, I kissed my father on his cheek.

"I love you, Dad." My voice was a soft whisper, but I knew he heard me.

Chapter 3

Blake

Where the fuck was she? I'd landed in Boise over two hours ago and taken a cab straight to Jen's house. The lights were on, but the house was vacant.

Sitting on the front step next to a large carved pumpkin leftover from Halloween, I tried her cell for the umpteenth time. No answer. And then I texted. Again no response. It was going on eight o'clock. The temperature had dropped significantly, and the damp Midwest autumn air sent a chill to my bones. My stomach rumbled with hunger as I hugged myself to keep warm.

Finally, a car pulled into the driveway. The headlights glared in my eyes; it was for sure Jen's dad's station wagon. Squinting, I jumped up as a familiar slim figure slid out of the driver's side door.

"Jen!" I sprinted up to her.

"Blake! Oh my God. What are you doing here?"

I searched her face. I could tell she'd been crying. Her green eyes were glazed and her thick layers of lashes were soaked. I took her in my arms and drew her close.

"I'm so, so sorry." Stroking her hair, I could only imagine what garbage Kat had told her.

Shivering, she leaned into me, resting her head against my leather jacket, her arms wrapped around me. "Oh, my love. Thank you for being here. It means so much to me." She began to sob softly.

I fluttered my eyes in confusion as I held and caressed her. "Tiger, why are you crying?"

"My Dad. He was hit by a car."

Holy. Fuck. Shit. I mentally hit the reset button. I had it all wrong. This was no time for me to tell her about Kat. And I wasn't even sure if Kat had contacted her.

"Jeez, Jen. I didn't know. Why didn't you call me or respond to my texts?"

"My cell phone died. And I don't have my charger. I'm sorry, baby."

Her snivels were gutting me. "No apologies necessary. How's your father?"

"Oh, Blake. It's not good. He may have sustained brain damage, and his leg is in bad shape. My mom's spending the night at the hospital."

"Fuck," I mumbled, bowing my head until my lips skimmed her scalp. Mr. McCoy had championed me when I was courting Jen, and I plain and simple adored him like a second father. I held her tighter.

A clap of thunder sounded. And a sudden downpour

fell upon us. The pitter of the heavy rain striking my leather jacket reverberated in my ears. I lifted up Jen's chin with my thumb. And crushed my lips against hers. Her hot tears mixed with the cold raindrops. Another burst of thunder exploded while my heart thundered too.

Believe it or not, I'd never kissed a girl in the rain before. Yet another first with my tiger. As the angry sky showered us with nature's tears, our lips melded together, our tongues entwined in a slow, sad dance.

Chapter 4

Jennifer

Blake filled me in on how he'd found out from Mrs. Cho that I'd flown to Boise. He'd been waiting for me on the front steps for more than two hours. After a long passionate kiss, I unlocked the front door and headed to the kitchen to whip up a quick dinner. We both hadn't eaten for hours and were famished. A beef casserole was in the refrigerator—probably the dinner my mother had prepared for my father. *His last supper?* While Blake washed up and changed into some dry clothes, I heated up the dish in the oven and choked back tears.

Blake met me in the dining room. "What's all this?" he asked as I padded in with some plates and silverware.

I eyed the dining room table where Blake and I had shared our first memorable Christmas Eve dinner almost a year ago. That magical snowy night he'd shown up at my doorstep to tell me he loved me. My heart was bursting with emotion. Lined up on the polished tabletop were hundreds of three inch square hand-painted frames encrusted with seashells and dusted with glitter. I set the china and silver on the credenza and made my way to the table. I picked up one of the charming frames. Inside it was an ivory place card with *Ms. Libby Clearfield*'s name elegantly scrolled in gold ink and printed below it: *Table 1.*

The rush of emotion surged through me. My creative mother, the ultimate DIY'er, had secretly taken it upon herself to make keepsake place card holders for all our wedding guests. *Oh, Mom!* My heart pitter-pattered, but then my moment of joy succumbed to an unbearable sadness. The dam holding back my tears broke loose, and I began to sob uncontrollably.

"They're place card holders my mom made for our wedding," I spluttered, my heart in my stomach. Now, everything was so up in the air.

Blake immediately took me in his arms and let me heave tears.

"Oh, Blake, I can't go through with this wedding if my dad's not there."

"Baby, we'll call it off. My mother will get over it. I'll do whatever you want to do. We're going to get through this together."

He tenderly kissed the top of my head, leaving his warm lips there as I continued to weep against his soft tee. His muscled arms held me tight. It felt so good to be blanketed in his warmth. His manliness. And his love.

After dinner, which we ate in the kitchen, we unwound in the living room. The beautiful plaid cashmere blanket Blake had given my father last Christmas was draped over Dad's favorite reading chair. The sight of it sent another ripple of sadness through me. In my mind's eye, I could see Dad reclining there with his reading glasses parked on his nose and a book in his hand. I had to blink my eyes several times to banish the illusion. And to blink back more tears.

While Blake plopped down on the comfy floral couch with his laptop to catch up on work-related e-mails, I meandered over to the easy chair. A thick, leather-bound volume of Shakespeare's sonnets was sitting on the cushion. The edges were frayed, indicating to me it had been read many times. Lifting it into my hand, I curled into the chair and wrapped myself in Blake's buttery blanket. There was something so comforting about being shrouded in this luxurious fringed cover, imbued with his love and my father's familiar pipe-smoker scent. I opened the book; it was a gift from my mother. The inscription was dated: *November 16, 1974.* My lips transitioned into a melancholic smile. The day my parents got married. Their fortieth anniversary was coming up soon. My eyes traveled down the page, and I drank in the words she'd written by hand:

To My Darling Husband~
My bounty is as boundless as the sea,
My love as deep; the more I give to thee,
The more I have, for both are infinite.
With eternal love~Meg

My eyes watered. I recognized the passage. It was from *Romeo and Juliet.* My dad, the English professor, and I shared a passion for Shakespeare, and I knew many of his brilliant lines by heart. These, in particular, resonated with me. I'd been struggling with writing an original marriage vow...and now I'd found it. The mention of the sea fit in well with the underwater theme of my wedding, and the fact that my mom had shared these beautiful words with my dad on their wedding day made them even more special. I began to leaf through the delicate yellowed pages of the book. As I read one exquisite sonnet after another, the words of another English poet whirled in my head. Chaucer.

If love is not, Oh God, what feel I so?
And if love is, what thing is it?

Shakespeare, however, did know what love is. My mother's chosen words softly formed on my lips.

Blake looked up from his computer. "Jen, are you okay?"

"Yes, baby." God, how I loved him. *Hear my soul speak. The very instant that I saw you did my heart fly to your service.* That first kiss. The first time ever I saw his face.

My eyes grew heavy. The next thing I knew I was in Blake's strong arms. He was carrying me upstairs. I must have dozed off. My sleepy gaze met his. Neither of us said a word.

Sometimes, words unspoken are the loudest. I knew Blake could intuit everything my weary mind was thinking. My love. My fear. My grief. He intermittently kissed my hair as we wound up the stairs.

When we crossed into my small bedroom, he set me down on my bed and tenderly undressed me, holding me in his gaze while he did. Our eyes never lost contact as he slid off my garments until I was fully unclothed. I sat motionless as Blake reverently cupped my breasts in his palms. And then he peeled off his clothes.

The first and last time Blake slept in my twin-sized bed, barely big enough for someone as petite as me, he'd fucked my brains out. Tonight was different. Bared to each other, he cocooned me in his arms, spooning me next to him. The warmth of his body blanketed my cold numbness.

On my side, I pressed my hands together. Closing my eyes, I silently prayed. *Oh, please God, make my dad okay. Please! For my mom. For me. For us.*

"Be brave, my tiger. It's going to be okay," Blake

whispered in my ear, holding me tight. His big warm hands folded over mine. A final round of tears made their way down my cheeks. Oh, Daddy! Oh, Mom! Oh, Blake!

The music of Blake's heartbeat and soft breaths lulled me to much needed sleep.

When Blake and I arrived at my dad's hospital room at seven the next morning, my mother was still sound asleep in an armchair, a small Bible folded over her lap. But Dad's hospital bed was gone. I gasped and clung to Blake, my worst fear rolling through me like a tidal wave. I began to breathe heavily and was close to hyperventilating.

In a state of panic, I woke my mom up, gently shaking her. "Mom, where's Dad?"

Startled, her eyes fluttered open. "Oh, Honey. Blake?"

Blake bent over and hugged my mom. "I'm so sorry to hear about your husband."

My heart was in my throat. "Mom, is he okay?"

"They took him for another MRI."

Relieved, my breathing calmed down. Blake and I took a seat on the cot that had been brought to the room. It looked as if my mother hadn't slept in it at all.

Blake drew me close to him and wrapped his arm

around my shoulders. I was wearing one of his heavy cashmere sweaters over the skirt I'd worn yesterday.

"Has there been any change in his condition?" I asked my mom as my husband-to-be soothingly brushed his long fingers along my upper arm.

She shook her head. Her usually wide blue-gray eyes were bloodshot slivers and her pale cheeks hollow. Purple shadows lined her lower lids. She looked like she'd gotten very little sleep. On a deep breath, she added, "But the good news is his vitals are stable."

I sighed another shaky breath of relief, but the worst wasn't over. We spent the next fifteen minutes making small talk to pass the time. After Blake told my mom how he'd found out I was in Boise, he offered to go to the cafeteria and bring back some coffee. Exhausted and drained, we were grateful.

"Mom, Blake called his sister last night, and she did some research. According to her colleagues at Cedars, Dr. Kumar is top notch. Dad's in good hands."

"I'm so glad to hear that. Blake is such a good man," my mother murmured. "And he adores you, my sweet girl."

A small smile flickered on my lips. "Yeah, Mom. I'm so lucky to have him. In many ways, he reminds me of Dad."

She smiled back. It was the first time I'd seen her smile since the accident.

Blake returned shortly with the coffee. Not the best

I'd ever had, but the strong bitterish brew instantly seeped into my veins and revitalized me. After a few sips, a clamor outside the room caught my attention. My eyes flew to the door. It was my father. Still hooked up to a portable IV unit, he was being wheeled back in. Holding a clipboard, the young doctor, who I'd met last night, accompanied the attendants and a nurse. With butterflies in my stomach, I watched as they reattached him to all the beeping machines.

I stood up and treaded to his bedside. Though the oxygen mask was off and he seemed to be breathing evenly on his own, his eyes were still shut. A light layer of graying stubble lined his peaceful face. My mother joined me. Her lips quivered as the nurse hooked him up to the last of the monitors. I squeezed her hand as Blake hovered behind me.

"Mrs. McCoy," began the doctor.

"Yes?" responded my mother, her voice trembling.

"I have good news for you and your daughter."

My rapidly beating heart was already dancing.

"The MRI shows the swelling in his brain has gone down. There's no permanent damage."

"Oh, dear Lord. Thank you!" Bursting into tears, my mother hugged the doctor. Whatever prayers she said must have worked. Tears of relief flooded my eyes too. Wrapping his arms around me from behind, Blake kissed the top of my head.

"When will he wake up?" I asked the doctor, leaning into Blake's hard body.

"It could be in a few minutes. Or in a few hours. Whenever he does, be sure to give him a little water." From the corner of my eye, I saw the nurse refill his plastic water cup on the nightstand next to his bed.

The doctor and his team excused themselves after telling us they'd be back later to check up on my dad. We returned to our seating positions, all keeping a vigilant watch on him. I gripped Blake's hand.

"Mom, I need to tell you something."

Her gaze shifted to me. A small smile played on her face, and serenity now filled her tired eyes. "What, honey?"

"On our way here, Blake and I had a discussion. We've decided to call off the wedding."

"Over my dead body, young lady."

The voice was a hoarse whisper but unmistakable. Dad!

He was awake and talking!

"Oh, Dad!" I ran over to his bed and kissed him, gushing with happiness.

My speechless, teary-eyed mother leapt up from her chair and caressed his face. "Oh, darling!" With the push of a button, she raised the bed just a smidgeon and lovingly held the cup of water to his lips.

"But Dad," I contested as he took a small sip through the straw. "You may not be well enough in time for the wedding."

"My Jennie, I have every intention of walking you down the aisle." He turned his bandaged head toward Blake. "And you, son, better be sure she's there."

"Yes, sir." They exchanged a conspiratorial wink.

My heart swelled with love for the two men I loved most in my life.

My beloved dad. And my soon-to-be husband.

Chapter 5

Blake

Knowing Jen's dad was going to be okay, I flew back to LA the next day. I had too much shit to take care of at work. Heading up a porn network came with its share of hard-ons and hardships. Jen, however, decided to remain in Boise until her father was released from the hospital later in the week. He was going home but would need a lot of physical therapy—especially since he was so intent on walking Jen down the aisle. I fucking loved this man.

I missed my tiger and was distracted. A weight hung over my head like a ticking time bomb. I still hadn't told Jen the truth about what had happened between Kat and me at the end of high school. I just couldn't break the news to her in Boise with what had happened to her father. I was certain it would make her an emotional wreck and dredge up all her trust issues. And knowing how Jen often overreacted, she might even call off the wedding—and break her father's heart and her mother's. And, last but not least, mine.

Every ring of my phone, ping in my mailbox, or

ding of a text made my nerves zing with anxiety and apprehension. At any time, I was expecting to hear from a hysterical Jen. That Kat had gotten to her. That she knew. But each time we spoke or texted, which was often, not one mention of Kat. I took one day at a time. Maybe, Kat hadn't been lying that afternoon at Saks and had no intention of sharing our past any further with Jen. I just couldn't be sure—she was a psycho bitch—and there was nothing I could do to stop her.

On Thursday, I had my weekly evening chat with my dad. True to fashion, we sat outside on my terrace and caught up over fine cigars and brandy. Unlike chilly Boise, the early November Los Angeles air was still balmy. Darkness, however, was descending.

"How's Jennifer's father doing?" asked my old man, after pouring the brandies.

I'd told my parents what had happen. Both were genuinely heartbroken and had not only called Mrs. McCoy but had also sent an array of exotic get-well flowers to his room that must have cost a small fortune. I filled my father in on the latest—that Harold had been released from the hospital and was determined to walk his little girl down the aisle.

My father chuckled and took another puff of his Cuban cigar. He blew out a curl of smoke. It faded into the night air. "I'm glad to hear that. If there's anything your mother and I can do to help, just let us know."

"Thanks, Dad." I smiled. My billionaire parents

were generous to a fault.

We imbibed our brandies in unison. My dad set his tumbler down on the round table between us. "So, how's the wedding shaping up?"

My father hadn't been involved. It was my mother's thing and he gave her total control. Not wanting to create any kind of friction between my parents, I hadn't told him about the issues we had with Enid and Katrina. Fucking Kat. The velvety brandy seeped through my veins and warmed me. It had been a stressful week, but now I was loosened up. The urge to tell my dad about Kat's antics burnt my tongue and the words tumbled out. My father listened intently, his lips pressed into a thin grim line. He plunked his tumbler down on the table again—this time with a loud, angry bang.

"You should have had security arrest her," he grumbled when I finished relaying the Saks incident. "She's pure trouble, that girl." Dad had never liked or trusted Kat despite the friendship between her mother and mine.

"Yeah, I should have." I took another sip of my brandy. "Dad, could you talk to Mom and try to get Kat out of our lives?"

My father flicked a thick layer of ashes into the Baccarat ashtray on the table. "Son, I don't think that's a good idea. It'll blow up in our faces. That crazy girl might go to the tabloids, and that's the last thing we all need."

My wise old man hated negative publicity. It wasn't good for our family or the company. Fortunately, the incident was handled in a way that had kept it out of the press all these years. I sucked in a deep breath. There was more than just negative publicity at stake.

"Dad, what if she tells Jennifer?"

My father's steel-gray eyes narrowed as he furrowed his bushy brows. "She doesn't know?"

I told him how I'd flown to Boise to tell her, but with Jen's dad's accident, it just wasn't the right time. And though Harold was now on the way to recovery, I didn't want to shake things up by phone or e-mail.

My understanding father nodded his head of silver hair. "When is she coming back?"

"Tomorrow." *Friday*.

"Skip Shabbat and take her out for a nice dinner. She's got to hear it from you. Don't waste any time."

My stomach twisted. Just as fast as my tiger had walked into my heart, just as fast she could walk out. "What if she—"

My father cut me short. "Blake, no amount of guilt can solve the past, and no amount of anxiety can change the future."

My old man's words of wisdom. I hoped he was right.

Friday couldn't get here soon enough or late enough. As much I coveted Jen in my arms—and in my bed—my stomach was in knots. Tonight, I was going to tell her the truth about my past with Kat. I wasn't sure how she was going to take it. Yes, the past was the past, and with Jen, I'd turned over a new leaf, but I'd kept it from her. My father had once said, there are two different types of sins: sins of commission and sins of omission. I'd committed both.

We touched base in the morning before she left for the airport. Upon landing, she was going straight to the set of *Bound to You*, the latest erotic romance we were shooting. She'd managed to score Jessica Chastain and Alexander Skarsgård to play the lead roles. I told her I wanted to meet her for dinner and picked a small romantic French restaurant not far from the set. I couldn't wait to hold her in my arms and fuck her brains out, but I had to get the truth out first. I owed it to her; she had to hear it from me. It was fucking killing me.

Shortly after I made an eight o'clock restaurant reservation, an unexpected e-mail showed up in my inbox. My chest tightened. Balls. It was from Kat and marked URGENT in shouty caps in the subject line. Fuck. Had she contacted Jen and told her the story? With apprehension, I opened it.

Dear Blake~

I'm really, really sorry about what happened at Saks last week as well as in Vegas. My behavior was totally out of line, and I would like to make it up to you. I hope you'll agree to meet me for a quick drink so I can apologize in person. There is also some important wedding detail I'd like to share with you. I'm planning a big surprise for Jennifer and I'd like to get your input. Please don't let me down. I hope you don't mind meeting at Greystone at 6:00 as I have dinner plans there immediately following with another client.

Yours~ Kat

My fingers drummed the keyboard while I stared at the e-mail. Should I agree to see her? Hear her out? Had *she* finally turned over a new leaf? Or was this just another ruse? Torn, I finally hit reply, driven by my curiosity to find out what surprise she had in mind for Jennifer. I typed three words: *See you there.* I could spend an hour or so with her and have time enough to meet Jen for dinner. While the bistro I'd chosen was not far from Greystone, traffic in LA on a Friday night was usually brutal, and I didn't want to be late. In the blink of an eye, Kat replied with a smiley face emoticon.

"Good to see you, Mr. Burns," said the flirty miniskirted blond hostess, who stood by the entrance to Greystone Manor. "I haven't seen you for a while."

The truth, though I still had a membership, I hadn't been back to the trendy club since the Conquest Broadcasting Christmas Ball last December. That night I'd fucked my tiger for the first time. Following that unforgettable night, I had no need for my fuck pad. I made a mental note to give it up permanently.

I told the attractive hostess I was here to meet Kat Moore. Smiling, she told me she was already here and led me through the uncrowded club (which wouldn't start filling up until much later). She deliberately swayed her hips. While her sexy walk got my attention, it didn't turn me on. I might still be a looker, but only one woman aroused me.

A big toothy smile flashed on Kat's face when she caught sight of me. She was seated at my regular table in the corner. There were plenty of empty tables in the vast club at this hour, but she'd chosen this one. An uneasy feeling settled in me. I was having second thoughts. Maybe agreeing to meet her here was a bad idea.

My skin prickling, I sat down facing her and crossed my legs under the table. Call it cock protection. My eyes took her in. Dressed in a strapless black dress, she looked, as usual, like a sophisticated goddess. Her wavy blond hair fanned over her broad shoulders, and she was perfectly made up. A bottle of champagne was anchored in an ice bucket beside the table. Kat was already sipping a fluteful of bubbly and had poured one for me.

"Blake, thank you for meeting me here on such short notice. I hope you don't mind I ordered a bottle of champagne."

She took a small sip. "Your favorite. Cristal."

"Actually, I appreciate it. I don't have much time. I've got to be somewhere at eight." I raised my crystal flute to my lips.

"Wait, Blake. Don't drink it until we toast to your wedding."

Hesitantly, I clinked my glass against hers, and as the crystal tinged, another smile slithered across her face. I guzzled my champagne as if it were soda water while she took another dainty sip. She then set her glass down and licked her upper lip.

"So what are you planning for Jennifer?" I asked, wanting to get straight to business. Her body language was unnerving.

She ran a hand through her thick mane of golden hair. "Oh, Blake. First things first. I'm terribly sorry for what happened in Vegas and at Saks. I spoke to my shrink about the incidents, and he insisted I apologize face to face. I hope you can forgive me."

"Apology accepted. Now what do you have in mind?" My words were rushed. Despite what sounded like sincerity, I wanted to get out of here as fast as I could.

Smiling, she circled the rim of her champagne flute with her long manicured finger. "Well, this is what I was thinking. Why don't we put together a video montage of you growing up to show at the wedding? I bet Jennifer would get a kick out of that."

I thought about the idea. Not a good one. I was sure even if I scrutinized it, Kat would find a way to slip in footage of the two of us. Especially Capri. I still didn't trust her one fucking bit.

"I don't think so. I'd prefer if you did one starring her."

"Blake, a wonderful idea." Still smiling, she paused. "And Blake—"

"Yes?"

"You have my word I won't ever tell Jennifer about our little secret. My lips are sealed." She slid her finger across her glossed lips.

I twitched a small grateful smile. "I really appreciate that, Kat."

Relieved, I reached into the ice bucket to refill my champagne glass. I fucking loved Cristal. A few more sips and I was out of here. Was I still going to tell Jen about the past? My thinking had grown cloudy.

As I poured the champagne into my flute, my hand shook. A sudden rush of nausea like I'd never known rose to my chest. The room began to spin. The bottle slipped out of my hand. I heard it shatter, and then everything faded to black.

Chapter 6

Jennifer

I got to Le Petit Café, the small intimate French restaurant where Blake had made a reservation, just a little before eight. I was the first to arrive, and the hostess showed me to our corner table. Blake knew how much I loved this restaurant with its candlelit, red-checkered-clothed tables and bistro menu; it reminded me so much of Paris where we'd filmed part of *Shades of Pearl*. Though we'd spoken and Skyped several times a day while I was in Boise, I was so eager to see Blake. I missed him terribly. My blood was streaming through me like champagne—happy little bubbles zapping me with giddiness.

Over a glass of Bordeaux, I perused the menu and thought about my day. It felt good to get back to work and be on a set. The filming of the first episode of the delightful Vanessa Booke's *Bound to You* had gone off without a hitch. I was so excited about this telenovela which we would be airing in the Fall. Today we had filmed the opening scenes that took place in Los Angeles. Rebecca, the spunky curvy heroine played by redhead Jessica Chastain, had said good-bye to her actor boyfriend Miles, played by Matt Bomer, after discovering he was cheating on her with his sexy co-star Scarlett—supermodel Kate Upton. The way Jessica had powerfully delivered the closing line—"I gave you everything, Miles, but you ripped it away. You chose her instead of me."—had me close to tears. My viewers were going to swoon over this adaptation of this popular erotic romance. Next week, pre-production started up in New York City where the rest of the filming would take place after the holidays. *After I got back from my honeymoon.*

The handsome, sandy-haired waiter, who looked to be an aspiring actor, came by and asked if I wanted an appetizer. Though ravenous, I passed and told him I was waiting for someone. I glanced down at my cell phone. It was 8:15. Blake should be here soon. He must be tied up in Friday night traffic. I called him. No answer.

Taking a small sip of the velvety red wine, I decided to catch up on e-mails. Intermittently, I called and texted Blake. Still no answer. I was growing edgy, and the wine did little to take the edge away. My eyes kept darting to the front of the restaurant, in hope of seeing Blake fly in.

It was now going on nine p.m. I was worried. Worried sick. Where was Blake? I called his cell phone every five minutes, but each time it went to his voicemail. I texted him. No response. I called his office and our home phone. No answer. I called Mrs. Cho and then his best friend Jaime, but they hadn't heard from him either and had no clue where he was. Mrs. Cho, however, did mention he'd left the office early for a meeting. *What meeting?* He hadn't mentioned one to me, and unfortunately, Mrs. Cho didn't know the details. *Strange.*

The server came by again to take my order. "I'm still waiting for someone," I told him glumly. With an irritated shrug, he marched off, leaving me alone. I tried all of Blake's numbers one more time, but still no Blake. A sudden chill ran through me. My heart hammered. Maybe something had happened to him. Like he'd gotten into a bad car accident. Or mugged. Maybe, I should call the police and all the local hospitals. Oh, God, please, please, please no! And then another equally horrible thought hit me with the force of an avalanche. His secret meeting. Blake always kept Mrs. Cho abreast of his whereabouts. My blood ran cold. Was he seeing someone else? Someone new he met while I was in Boise? All my insecurities and trust issues flooded my brain, and nausea rushed to my chest.

My cell phone pinged. An e-mail. From Blake? I glanced down at the screen. It was from the last person I wanted to hear from. Kat. She was probably just e-mailing me to confirm my fitting appointment tomorrow. With reluctance, I opened it. The body of the message was all of two words: *Please review.*

There were several attachments. All jpegs. Brides-maid dresses? Seating arrangements? The latest tropical fish that would be swimming in the Bernsteins' salt-water pool?

While I was in no mood for wedding detail, I opened the attachments, one at a time. My heart fell to my stomach. And all air left my lungs. The phone shook in my trembling hands.

"Oh my God," I heard myself say as I viewed one photo after another of Blake and Kat bared to each other and entwined in a familiar bed. The satin-sheeted one in his fuck pad at Greystone Manor—where he'd fucked me for the first time the night of the Conquest Broadcasting Christmas party. The photos ranged from heated embraces to Kat sucking his cock. And so much more. By the fifth photo, I'd had enough. Scorching tears poured down my face. Oh my God. How could I be so blind? In so much denial? Reality hit me like a crashing meteor. Blake was still into her.

The server came by again. "Have you decided what you want to order? The kitchen will be closing down soon."

I looked up at him with my tear-flooded eyes. "I-I'm sorry. I won't be staying for dinner." My voice was a mere rasp. Barely a whisper.

The server regarded me with compassion. I guess he'd seen a lot of girls stood up in his time. But none as crestfallen as me.

"No problem, madame."

Madame. The French word for "Mrs." Mrs. Blake Burns was not in my stars.

"Thank you for understanding." I dug through my bag and found my wallet. I pulled out a hundred-dollar bill. The hundred-dollar bill Blake had given me when I'd stripped for him in that seedy motel; I'd kept it as emergency money. This was an emergency of the worst kind. I plunked it down on the table.

"I'll be right back with your change," the sweet waiter said.

"No need," I stammered. While my glass of wine came to only twelve dollars, the hardworking server deserved the money for his time, patience, and compassion.

"Are you sure?" His eyes lit up with surprise.

"Yes, please." I rose from my seat, my knees so weak I thought I'd fall down. The kindly waiter pulled out my chair and helped me up.

"Merci, madame. I hope you have a lovely evening."

That wasn't happening.

I don't know how I made it back to Blake's condo. Tears blurred my vision, and twice I almost got into a major auto accident. The ache in my heart was so great I thought I might have a coronary. First, Bradley. Now, Blake. But the pain this time was exponentially worse. Unbearable. I needed windshield wipers to wipe my tears away.

Fortunately, Blake's condo was not far from the restaurant, and traffic along Wilshire Boulevard was light. I got there in no time. I valeted my car, skirted past the doorman, and hurried upstairs. I made a couple of calls, and then collapsed onto the couch. I could no longer share Blake's bed. It was already ancient history. Tomorrow, I would be gone.

You chose her instead of me.

Chapter 7

Blake

"Fuck," I heard myself murmur. *Fuck, fuck, fuck.* My head was spinning; my mouth felt like the Mohave Desert, and nausea consumed me. Slowly, I peeled my eyes open—well to be honest, only one. It took me several long, nauseating moments to realize where I was. I was in my Greystone fuck pad, sprawled naked on my bed. I had no fucking idea how I'd gotten here, and the shitfaced way I felt didn't make remembering any easier. I glanced at my watch. Squinting with the one opened eye, I made out the time. It was six o'clock. Except in my windowless suite, I had no idea if it was six in the morning or the evening.

The bed was a rumpled mess with the covers half off, and I noticed my clothes were strewn on the floor. How did they get there? How did I get here? I hadn't been back to my fuck pad since the time I'd fucked Jennifer at the office Christmas party. And that was almost a year ago.

I crawled out of bed. In my sorry state, I could barely stand up. My legs felt like Jell-O and another tidal wave of nausea descended on me. Close to passing out, I collapsed onto the floor and crawled on my hands and knees to the adjacent bathroom. Frankly, I wasn't sure I'd make it to the toilet in time, but thank fucking God I did. Perched on my knees, I puked my guts out until my throat burned and my insides were torn. Believe it or not, I actually felt a little better. And despite my headache the size of Texas, a little more clear-headed. But I still couldn't piece together how I'd gotten here or what had happened in the last twenty-four hours.

I managed to get to my feet and noticed my cock was flaccid. I'd never woken up without a big boner. Poor Mr. Burns was as wasted and confused as I was. This was bad. Really bad. I quickly brushed my teeth and then staggered out of the bathroom after passing on a hot shower. I didn't think I was steady enough. One glance in the bathroom mirror confirmed that. I looked like death warmed over. Like someone had painted me with chalk and left me in Death Valley to die. Roadkill.

Back in my fuck pad, I gathered up my suit in slo-mo. I slipped on my dress shirt first, unable to button it with my shaky hands. Then the slacks and jacket. At last minute, I threw my tie around my neck. In a moment of panic, I slipped my hand into my slacks pocket where I kept my wallet and cell phone. To my relief, both were there. I pulled out my cell phone, and immediately checked my texts, e-mails, and phone messages. There were dozens. All from one person. My

Jen—wondering where I was and asking me to call her. I immediately speed-dialed her number, but there was no response. I texted her and e-mailed her. Zilch again. Maybe it was six o'clock in the morning and she was still sleeping. And then an unnerving thought punched me in the gut—I hadn't gone home to her. What could she be thinking?

Without warning, my cell phone died on me. I stared at it blankly. What did it matter?

I didn't have an explanation.

Chapter 8

Jennifer

My sleep was tearful and restless. I don't know why I bothered. I fumbled for my cell phone, which was tucked under my pillow, and glanced at the screen. It was going on five a.m. If it weren't such an ungodly hour, I would have called Libby or Chaz or even my parents. I had the burning urge to talk to someone. Anyone. Blake had never called or texted me. Shutting my eyes, I tried to fall back to sleep on the couch, but it was futile. My throat was raw from crying, and the ache in my heart was palpable.

Light shortly filtered through the floor-to-ceiling windows. My burning eyes took in the dawn of another day in LA. Beautiful as usual, but not beautiful for me. In a few hours, I would be on a plane. Away from LA and the man I thought I loved with my body and soul. Except he'd betrayed me. I pulled the blanket over my head, and then forcing myself off the couch, I stumbled to the bedroom Blake and I shared. Or should I say once shared. My eyes stinging, I gazed at the king-sized bed where we had made beautiful, endless love countless times. There was no more "we." Painfully, I retrieved a small suitcase from the walk-in closet and tossed it onto the duvet. I needed to pack. I was going back home. To be with my parents who needed me— but only a fraction of how much I needed them.

Halfway done packing, I heard the door to the apartment unlock. And then I heard it slam shut. A shiver skittered though me. Blake! I continued tossing a week's worth of clothing into my suitcase. While I hadn't informed HR of my sudden leave of absence, I was positive I could convince them I could work from Boise, given my stellar job performance. MY SIN-TV ratings were though the roof. And right now, most of our telenovelas were in post-production, not immediately demanding my attention. I just wasn't going to tell them that most of my time would be spent looking for a new job.

I heard a shuffle of heavy footsteps approach. I ignored them. I was almost packed. And then he called out to me.

"Jen." His voice sounded worn and hoarse.

I refused to acknowledge him and continued with my packing. Every muscle clenched. The pain was so great. Treacherous tears cascaded down my face.

"Jen," he murmured again, this time, his voice a desperate croak.

I couldn't help but face him as he staggered my way. I soaked him in with my watering eyes. He looked awful. His hair was a wild mess, and his complexion had a ghoulish green cast. His suit was wrinkled, his creased shirt opened, and his tie hung loosely and unevenly around his neck.

"Where are you going?" he rasped, eyeing my suitcase.

"Home." I stabbed the word at him and impulsively tugged at my engagement ring. My finger swollen, the damn thing wouldn't budge. I was going to have to mail it to him.

He gazed at me imploringly, his bloodshot eyes blinking for an explanation.

"I'm moving out, Blake."

"Why, tiger? Why?"

I answered his question with another a question. A Jewish thing to do, so I'd learned. "Where were you last night?"

He shook his head. "I don't fucking know."

Bullshit. I tossed my cell phone at him. He caught it…barely. His reflexes were not what they normally were. Of course. Kat had fucked his brains out.

"Just click the first e-mail. And then any attachment. I'm sure they'll trigger your memory."

My eyes stayed fixed on him as he did as asked. His glazed eyes grew round.

Raking his hand though his disheveled hair, he groaned, "What the fuck?"

"What do you mean?"

"What I mean is I have no recollection of being with the bitch."

The angry way he said "bitch" struck a deep chord. His gaze met mine. I swiped at my tears.

"Honestly, tiger, I have no memory of the last twenty-four hours. Everything's a blank."

His sunken eyes bore into me like a puppy looking for love. I searched them, seeking the truth.

"I swear to God, Jen. You have to believe me."

My inner conscience went into war-mode. There was the me who distrusted and the me who wanted to believe. My mind was a battlefield. But, one by one, the soldiers of distrust were being knocked down by the true believers. A mental massacre led by my courageous heart. I cupped Blake's stubbled face in my hands and faced him squarely. His sister's warning about Kat resounded in my head. *Don't let her manipulate you.*

"Blake, I believe you." My voice was soft but solid. This was a big step forward for me in the trust department. Dr. Williams, my support group leader, would be proud of me.

He blinked his eyes in disbelief. "You do?"

"I do. Are you okay?"

"I feel like fucking crap. Like I have a major hangover. Everything's so hazy."

My poor baby. I wrapped my arms around him and drew him close to me. He held me against him, my head resting on his heart. The heart that belonged to me.

"I think the bitch must have gotten me drunk, but I seriously don't remember what drink I ordered. Or how many."

"Did you blackout?"

"I must have. But I've never done that before."

I digested Blake's words and his condition. He had some form of amnesia. In my rape support group, there were a couple of girls who unknowingly had been drugged at a bar and then date raped. When they woke up naked in a strange bed or in a dark alley, their rapist was long gone, and they had no memory of what had happened.

I had a hunch. Fucking Kat had drugged him and virtually raped him. What a sick chick! I was going to prove it and have my revenge.

"Come on, baby. Let me give you a bath. And then we're going to your doctor."

"I don't need to go to a doctor. I just need to rest and be with you."

"Baby, I want to make sure you're all right. And I have a theory I want to prove. It's going to take a test."

Reluctantly, Blake agreed. I helped him off with his clothes and then led him to the bathtub.

Chapter 9

Blake

I felt fucking violated by the fucking bitch. Dirty, used, and abused even though I couldn't remember a goddamn thing. The thought of Kat having her mouth any place on my body, let alone my dick, sickened me. I only belonged to one woman. My tiger who was kneeling by the tub and washing away the vague memories of last night. How could I let myself drink my way to submission and oblivion? Hadn't I learned my lesson? I leaned my head against the tub and squeezed my eyes closed, soaking in the guilty pleasure of the tender touch of the woman I loved. And could have lost.

"How do you feel?" asked Jennifer, helping me out of the tub. She draped a large fluffy towel around me.

"Fucked up."

The bath had helped only a little. Waves of nausea still rolled in my chest; my head was spinning, and I was experiencing coordination problems. Even buttoning my jeans was a challenge. Jen helped me get re-dressed and insisted on driving me to our family doctor's office in Beverly Hills. God bless her. I was seriously in no condition to drive.

I tried to think straight. How was I going to handle this mess? Pointing the finger at Kat had all kinds of repercussions—from an unwanted scandal to a rift between my mother and hers. The wedding itself could be jeopardized.

"Jen, I don't want to go through with this," I protested as she pulled her Kia into the parking structure of the medical building where Dr. Klein, an internist, had an office. He had been our family physician for years and had a very close relationship with my parents as well as my sister.

"You have to. For yourself. And for me," she retorted in search of a parking spot. "We need proof that Kat drugged you."

"Drugged me?" My voice rose an octave.

"Yes." She shot the word at me, without giving me a chance to contest it.

"What do I have to do?" I could take a bullet for Jen, but the thought of a long needle being inserted into my flesh freaked me out. I could be such a wuss.

"Not much. Just pee in a little cup."

I inwardly sighed with relief, but the outstanding issues weighed on my chest. "What if it comes back positive?"

"Then we'll know." Her voice was matter-of-fact.

"But what if Dr. Klein starts asking all kinds of

questions?"

"You're just going to tell him that you don't remember a thing."

"Are you going to tell Kat's mother?" That would certainly create hell.

"Not if I don't have to. But I'm going to need your help."

My tiger shot me a mischievous smile as she pulled into a parking spot. Somehow, I knew her creative juices were flowing.

Dr. Klein's office was packed, but he was able to squeeze me in with only a short wait. Jen accompanied me to the examining room and made me take a seat on the examining table. She sat down in a close-by armchair.

"Do you want to play nursie?" I asked, my sense of humor trickling back. Perhaps to mask my stress.

"You wish."

Oh did I. The thought of her in a tight little nurse's uniform giving me a physical—touching me everywhere that needed touching—sent a tiny jolt to my cock. At least, my manhood was intact. Or so I thought. Maybe next Halloween I'd buy her a costume and I could live out my fantasy.

My fantasy came to an abrupt halt when Dr. Klein

strode into the small sterile room. A kindly looking man in his mid fifties, he was holding a clipboard and wearing a stethoscope around his neck.

"Well, hello, Blake. What brings you here today?" He gave me the once-over. "You look a little under the weather. A touch of the flu?"

Jen chimed in. "No, Doctor. He just needs to give you a urine sample, and we need the results back today if possible."

Dr. Klein lifted a brow. "And you may be?"

"Jennifer McCoy. Blake's fiancée. Nice to meet you."

"Nice to meet you too, Jennifer. My wife and I got your lovely wedding invitation. We'll be there."

Jennifer smiled. "Wonderful."

Dr. Klein winked at her. "So did our boy have a little too much sex and get a urinary tract infection?"

"Not exactly, Doctor," I replied. "But I need to have my pee tested for anything unusual."

Doctor Klein's eyes narrowed, creating a deep crease between them. "Blake, are you doing drugs? Cocaine? Ecstasy?"

"No, sir. But I think I may have been drugged."

"That's very serious, Blake. Can you tell me more?"

I remembered Jen's instructions and shook my head. "I don't remember a thing."

With resignation, he took my blood pressure and then listened to my heart. His brows furrowed. "Your heartbeat is erratic and your blood pressure is abnormally low."

Fuck. Maybe I was going to die.

He put the stethoscope to my back and asked me to take a few deep breaths.

"And your breathing is somewhat labored. How do you feel?"

"To be honest, I feel like crap. Sluggish, nauseous, and dizzy."

"Anything else?"

Again, Jen chimed in. "He's having difficulty with his motor skills."

The doctor listened intently. "Like what?"

"Like unbuttoning his jeans."

The doctor shot her a wry look. "I would imagine Mr. Burns is usually very good at that."

Jennifer's face flushed while I let out a small laugh.

"Very well." He ambled over to the sink counter and retrieved a lidded plastic cup sealed in a sanitary wrapper. He handed it to me. "The bathroom is down the hall. I'd like you to fill up the cup at least halfway."

I'd been through this routine for my annual physicals. I had to hold my big cock and aim. The rim of my dick was bigger than that of the cup. This time, I didn't want to do it alone.

"Um, uh, Doctor. Jennifer's right. I'm having a lot of trouble buttoning and unbuttoning my jeans. Can she come with me?"

"I don't see why not. But both of you be sure to wash your hands first. When you're done, just print your name on the label with the marker that's on the shelf, and leave it there. We'll try to get the results back to you in a few hours. There's a urologist I know who owes me a favor."

I jumped off the examining table. "It's pee time."

Jen looked at me sheepishly. "Do I really have to come?"

"Yes. You have to come." I gestured toward the door, my very naughty mind already back in business.

A short minute later, we were huddled in the small, functional bathroom. After we washed our hands, I tore off the cellophane wrapping of the cup and removed the lid.

"Jen, this is going to be a team effort. Unbutton my jeans."

Silently, she did as bid. I'd gone commando. The little rise I'd gotten from my nursie fantasy was long gone. My heavy cock hung low.

"Now baby, grip my dick and aim it into the cup." Her warm hand clamped the lower third. There was a lot more I wanted her to do with it than play fire hydrant, but truthfully, I wasn't sure I could get it up. A terrifying thought sent a shudder through me. Fuck. Did I have permanent damage?

"Am I doing it okay?" Jen asked hesitantly, breaking into my disconcerting thoughts.

"You're doing just great, baby. Here goes."

On the next breath, I shot a stream of pee into the cup. It wasn't quite the same as shooting my load with Jennifer's hand wrapped around my cock, but it felt good. I'd never peed with a girl before. It was strangely sexy. I wanted to reward Jen for believing me. After labeling the cup and sealing it with the lid, I placed it on a shelf with a row of other used cups. Jen commended me.

"Good job, Blake. We should wash up."

I squirted some of the liquid soap onto my palms. Jen followed suit, but while she did, I folded my arms around her tiny waist.

In a rapid heartbeat, I unbuttoned her jeans and slid them down her legs. My small motor skills were improving. I slipped a soaped-up hand under the band of her lacy panties and then lubricated her folds. I watched her lips part and her head arch back in the mirror above the sink.

"Blake! What are you doing?" she breathed out.

"Thanking you properly for believing me. And for coming here with me."

"Oh!"

I began to caress her slick pussy and soon felt her heat. I had to make this quick. Before Dr. Klein sent someone to check on me. Hastily, I moved my fingers to her clit and circled it vigorously. She bit down on her bottom lip to suppress her sounds though sexy little whimpers lodged in her throat. Her breathing was uneven. Enjoying every minute, I nuzzled the back of her neck.

"Oh, God. You're making me come!"

"That's the plan," I breathed into her ear, rubbing my cock against her backside with the hope I'd get an erection. Fuck. Nothing. Not even a little twitch. I refocused my energy on Jen, rubbing her nub harder.

"Oh, Blake," she moaned as she bucked against me, her pussy trembling and spilling with her juices.

I planted a chaste kiss on her head and just held her. "Thanks again for *coming,* tiger. I needed you here with me."

"Blake, I'm always going to be there for you."

"The same, baby. The same."

Her dreamy smile met mine in the mirror, and then we headed back to the examination room where we took our former positions. Dr. Klein returned shortly.

"Did you have difficulty urinating, Blake?" he asked. "You were in the bathroom for quite a while."

"No, Doc. Not at all. A little rough at the beginning. I'm not used to peeing in a cup. But once I got it going, no problem." But the truth, there was a problem. A big one. Or should I say a not so big one, depending on how you looked at it and put it into perspective. I couldn't get an erection. I desperately wanted to tell him about it, but I held my tongue.

With a smile, he nodded. "Good. And I must say

you're looking a little better than when you first came in. I suggest you go home and rest and keep your jeans buttoned until we have the results of your test. I'll call you as soon as I get them."

I stood up from the examining table and joined Jennifer. Dr. Klein turned to face us.

"And Jennifer, a pleasure to meet you. Congratulations on your engagement. I look forward to the wedding."

Jennifer beamed. "We look forward to seeing you there."

"Ditto." I shook the good doctor's hand and thanked him for seeing me.

Silently, I thanked Jennifer for believing me and not calling the whole thing off. I still didn't know how I was going to handle Kat who was out to sabotage us. Or the new, potentially life-changing problem I faced, thanks to her.

I fucking loved my tiger.

And fucking hated that bitch.

Chapter 10

Jennifer

I wanted Blake to rest. Doctor's orders. It was Saturday, hence no need for either of us to go into the office. So I made him put on his pajamas and tucked him into bed. Then, I heated up the leftover matzo ball soup I'd made and frozen a few weeks ago. He said he wasn't hungry, but I forced him to eat it. In fact, I fed it to him, lovingly blowing on each tablespoon before putting it to his lips. Blake, it seemed, was always taking care of me. The role reversal felt so good. I loved taking care of my man. *That* man who loved me so. He told me he felt a little better after finishing the bowl of the nourishing broth. I smiled. Blake's grandma was right: matzo ball soup was Jewish penicillin as much as it was an aphrodisiac. Blake, however, was in no condition for a romp.

I joined him in bed, snuggling close to him. I flipped on the TV to get our minds off the results of the urine test. In the middle of a *SpongeBob* episode, Blake's cell phone rang. It was Dr. Klein. I asked Blake to put the phone on speaker mode. My heartbeat sped up with anticipation.

"Blake, we got back the results of the urine sample," began Dr. Klein.

"And..." Blake sounded anxious. I clasped his hand.

"Everything is normal except..." The doctor paused. "The lab found a high level of Rohypnol."

"What's that?"

"It's the brand name for flunitrazepam, a drug that is commonly used in drug-facilitated sexual assaults. Otherwise known as the date-rape drug."

There was silence on Blake's end. His lips tightened into a grim, angry line. I knew what he was feeling. I was feeling it too. A maelstrom of rage and abuse.

The doctor continued. "Blake, this is very serious. It's considered a crime. Do you have any recollection of who did this to you?"

Blake drew in a sharp breath. "Doctor, like I told you before, I don't. I went to a club, the one I belong to, and had a cocktail at the bar. Someone must have slipped it into my drink."

I gave his hand a little squeeze, letting him know he'd handled the inquiry perfectly. The doctor responded.

"Well, Blake, I still think you should report it. And let me tell you, you're very lucky. The high dose of Rohypnol mixed with alcohol could have killed you."

A shiver ran through me from my head to my toes.

The thought of Kat taking Blake away from me forever was unfathomable. I squeezed his hand tighter, never wanting to let go of him.

Maintaining his composure, Blake told Dr. Klein he would think about it and then took another deep breath. "One thing, Doctor. I hope you'll share none of this with my parents or sister."

"Of course not, Blake. Doctor-patient privilege."

"Thanks."

"Of course. One last question, how do you feel?"

"Better but still queasy."

"That's normal. I want you to rest and drink plenty of fluids. By tonight, the drug should be out of your system."

"I will." Blake paused, placing his free hand on the duvet close to his cock. It had been very still today. A look of uncertainty washed over his face. "Doc, will this flu-nit-shit-whatever drug have any long-term effects on my uh...um...equipment?"

I heard the good doctor chuckle. "No, Blake. You should be absolutely fine."

Blake blew out a breath of relief. Inwardly, I did the same.

With that, the two exchanged good-byes and Blake ended the call. He hastily tossed his phone onto the bed and then turned to look at me. His look of relief had turned to rage.

"The fucking bitch!"

I gently cradled his embittered face in my hands, turning it toward me. "Baby, the good news is you're going to be okay."

Taking me in his arms, Blake thanked me again for trusting him and for making him take the test. But he was still mad as hell. What was most infuriating him was that he didn't know what do next. He explained all the ramifications of taking Kat down. Exposing her. Moreover, Kat most likely still had all the photos on her phone and could use them to spin more evil.

He slammed his fist against the bed. "Fucking, fucking bitch."

Thank God, for the cushy memory foam mattress (we'd never bought a springy one) because on any other surface, Blake would have likely broken some bones with the force of his fist. I lifted the hand to my lips and tenderly kissed the back of it.

"Fucking, fucking bitch," he muttered again.

"No, baby, *fuck* the bitch." My father had always preached, "Don't get mad. Get even."

I told Blake my idea without giving away too many details. And that I needed his help. "I trusted you, baby. Now, you must trust me."

"I do, tiger."

After a sweet kiss, he did as I asked and made two calls. Yes! Things were working out.

Sucking in air through his nose, he set the phone down on the bed and asked me to face him. His large hands took hold of my shoulders. He looked anxious.

"Jen, there's something I've got to tell you about Kat. About our past that I should have told you before."

My pulse sped up and my eyes fluttered. He hadn't been honest with me?

He took in a shaky breath and on the exhale he simply said, "I got Kat pregnant."

My heart skipped a beat. "You have a child?"

"No, tiger." And then a long tense pause. "She had a miscarriage."

"When did this happen?" Though shocked, I kept my tone even-keeled.

"The summer after high school. We were at some graduation party, and I got drunk. As always, she was all over me. Stupid me succumbed. The fucking condom must have torn from her nails, and I guess she was off birth control."

"Jeez."

"Jen, she wanted to keep the baby so I would marry her. My parents were up in arms. Rightfully, neither of them thought we should do that. We were too young. I wanted nothing to do with her, and believe me, the last fucking thing I wanted was to be a father at the age of eighteen. Her parents, however, wanted us to marry. The recession had hurt them, and they were going through lean times. If Kat married me, they would no longer have to support her extravagant lifestyle, and they could smooch off my parents, who had protected their investments. So, they supported Kat's decision. I was fucked. Afraid of a scandal that would embarrass my family, I lied and told her I'd marry her if she kept my identity under wraps until the baby was born. She went along with it, taunting me each day she would break her promise if she caught me with another girl."

Blake had stunned me in into silence. Wordlessly, I listened on. His voice faltered.

"Six months in and barely showing—her friends thought she'd just gained weight—the bitch went horseback riding." Blake paused, taking a breath. "She went into labor. My sister was discreetly there for her, but the baby was stillborn."

"Oh, Blake!" So, that was what Marcy was hiding. I cupped my petite hand over his large one, still splayed on my shoulder. Raw emotion poured through my veins as he went on.

"It was a boy. We had a proper Jewish burial for him and had to name him. Gabriel…after an angel."

The angel of revelation.

"Just our families attended." Blake's voice softened, and he closed his eyes for a long moment as if he were going back in time.

"Jen, I'll never forget that day and that tiny shoe-box-sized coffin being lowered into the earth. My little mistake. As our rabbi recited the *Kaddish,* the prayer for the dead, it began to drizzle, and the anger I had toward Kat turned inward. I hated myself and grieved for the little boy I didn't want or would never know. With each shovel of the earth, I grew numb. Kat didn't shed a tear. At the end of the service, she spat in my face and called me an asshole."

He bowed his head. "She was right. I was an asshole. A stupid fucking asshole."

"Blake, look at me." Slowly, he lifted his eyes. "You're *not* an asshole."

My heart was cracking. This story explained so much of Blake. His fear of relationships. And his baby-phobia. My mind flashed back to the lunch we had last year with Jaime and how uncomfortable he initially was with his twins. And then to his uncomfortable reaction to my pregnancy test. The story wasn't over.

"After the burial, Kat had a breakdown. Maybe from a hormone imbalance, depression, or guilt. Or a combination of all three. She tried to commit suicide and her parents institutionalized her. A year later, she was released, and the first thing she did was show up at my UCLA dorm and tell me how much she loved me. One night, she even managed to break in, and I found her naked in my bed. I had to get a restraining order. Fortunately, she went to live abroad but returned to LA last fall. Jen, to make a long story short, she hasn't stopped stalking me. The girl is sick. Poison. I just wish I'd told all of this to you sooner."

"Why didn't you?" My voice was tender, my eyes compassionate.

"I wanted to. She stalked me in Vegas and threat-ened to tell you herself."

My blood simmered. Did she hit on him?

"I wanted to tell you the minute I came back, but I couldn't with the way you were feeling. Then, the day you went to see Marcy, she fucking assaulted me again at Saks. I thought she'd gotten to you when I couldn't reach you. That's why I flew to Boise. But when I found out about your dad, I just couldn't bring myself to tell you. I didn't need to lay this heavy shit on you and upset you more."

I held his face in my hands and gazed lovingly into his remorseful eyes. He had made the right decisions.

"And then I was going to tell you last night at din-ner. And the psycho bitch fucked me over again." His eyes burnt into mine. "Can you forgive me, tiger?"

"There's nothing to forgive, my love. It wasn't your fault. It was a nightmare you had no control over. We just can't hide things from each other."

Silently, he nodded in my palms, and I acknowl-edged him with a smile on my lips and in my eyes.

"Blake, baby, I love you so much. Do you believe me?"

He drew me tight against him, and the hot, passion-ate kiss he planted on my lips was all I needed.

Fraught with emotion, I lay in bed with Blake until he dozed off. Quietly, I slipped away and booted up my computer. It was time to take the sick bitch down. For all the pain she'd caused me. And for all she'd caused my Blake. I typed away.

To: Katrina Moore
From: Jennifer McCoy
Subject: Meeting/URGENT

Dear Kat~

I am writing you with tears in my eyes. I am completely devastated by the photos you sent me of you and Blake.

You were absolutely right. Blake is still into you. How could I have been so blind? And so foolish for trusting him with my heart and my life?

I have no choice but to end our engagement and call off the wedding. I've already given him back his ring. With all due respect for his family, I would very much like to meet with you discreetly tomorrow to discuss how we can best break the news to all involved. I am temporarily staying at a bungalow at The Beverly Hills Hotel, which, at least, Blake had the decency to put me up in. I would appreciate if you could meet me there.

I never thought I would thank you, but I owe

you my deepest gratitude. Though sadness fills every crevice of my being, it is better to know now where I stand with Blake than to have had my heart broken by him after our union. I can only hope he does not do the same to you.

With my sincerest appreciation~ Jennifer

I reread my e-mail. I loved writing every single word. With a wicked smile, I hit send. Just like I thought…I instantly got a response.

To: Jennifer McCoy
From Katrina Moore
Subject: Meeting/URGENT

Dear Jennifer—

My heart bleeds for you. What Blake did is appalling and I am partly accountable. In all fairness, I tried to warn you. His feelings for me are strong and real. In fact, he just called me and informed me about your breakup. He can't wait to get back together with me. He ended the call by saying that I was his first and only true love.

Yes, I agree we should meet tomorrow. Let's make it 3 p.m. I'll come directly to your bungalow and we'll strategize an exit plan. Thank you for trusting me.

Yours truly—Katrina

Perfection! I confirmed the meeting. A fiendish grin whipped across my face. My newest production, *Fuck the Bitch*, was underway. It was now time to recruit my co-producer and co-stars. Grabbing my cell phone, I made two calls, one right after the other.

Lights! Camera! Action! Everything was in place. Tomorrow could not come fast enough.

Blake had made arrangements for the bungalow—the same one my parents had stayed at during their visit. It was permanently leased by Conquest Broadcasting and used for visiting dignitaries, investors, and out-of-town producers, directors, and stars. Luck was on our side—it was vacant.

I headed over to The Beverly Hills hotel at lunchtime, leaving my car with the valet. The pink stucco bungalow, located in a very secluded area of the property, couldn't have been more perfect—consisting of an elegantly appointed living room, bedroom, and kitchenette. Soon afterward, my partner in crime, Libby, showed up. She was beaming with excitement.

"You're a fucking genius, girl," she exclaimed, tossing her canvas bag onto the plush Hollywood Regency-styled couch.

"Hope it works," I replied. "Pussy and her girlfriend should be here any minute."

Pussy was Pussy Amour, the co-star of SIN-TV's highly rated prime time show, *Private Dick*. She had recently created a stir in the porn world after revealing she was gay. To the industry's surprise, the fact she was a lesbian only helped the show's ratings. Pussy had some very special talents as did her girlfriend whose name was Swell.

Libby and I were drinking some Diet Cokes when the doorbell rang. I leapt up from the couch to open the door. Sure enough, it was my expected guests.

Pussy, who I'd gotten to know from various conventions, gave me a big hug. I introduced her to Libby and she introduced us to Swell.

Both women were wearing tight-ass jeans, mile-high platforms, and tanks that clung to their planet-sized boobs. Each was a carrying a small overnight bag though they were returning to Vegas in the evening. Bearing a striking resemblance to Pink with their short spiked platinum hair, they could practically be sisters except Swell had piercings all over as well as sleeves of colorful tattoos along her arms.

"Thanks for coming," I said, ushering them into the main room.

"Anything for you and Blake," responded Pussy. "Are you ready to take the bitch down?"

I drew in a gulp of air. "Yes, but I'm nervous."

"There's nothing to be worried about, honey." She shot her companion a flirtatious wink. "Come on,

Swell, baby. Let's get ready and set things up."

Taking their bags with them, they ambled arm in arm to the bedroom. Five minutes later they re-appeared.

"Holy shit!" exclaimed Libby, her jaw as wide opened as mine.

Both women were clad in matching black leather bustiers, fishnets, and stilettos. Tattoos were every-where on Swell's body. Pussy had one, too, of a sex kitten by her shoulder.

"I'm so ready for the Pussy-Kat show," purred the porn star. She let out a ferocious meow and mock-swiped her claws.

I went over the plan with them. Everyone knew what to do. At close to three o'clock, Pussy and Libby flattened themselves against the wall on either side of the bungalow entrance. Swell was in the bedroom. At exactly three, the doorbell rang. My heartbeat sped up. Showtime!

Wasting no time, I swung open the door halfway. Standing before me was Kat, dressed to kill in a tight-fitting designer silk dress that accentuated her D-cup boobs.

"Hi, Kat," I said in my most despondent voice, even adding in a sniffle. "Let me take your bag."

With a smug smile, she handed me her monstrous purse and stepped inside the bungalow.

"Where would you like—"

Before she could finish her question, Pussy and Libby ambushed her. Pussy seized her arms while Libby grabbed her stiletto-clad feet by the ankles.

"What the fuck?" she shrieked. "What are you doing to me?" Writhing and kicking, she continued to rant as Pussy and Libby hauled her into the bedroom.

"Thanks for coming, Kat," I said brightly, trailing behind them, her handbag slung over my arm.

In no time, we were in the bedroom, and Kat was flat on her back on the bed. Libby and I pinned her down while Pussy and Swell worked together to fasten the pink leather restraints on her wrists and ankles.

"You can't do this to me!" she growled, the restraints quickly in place. "I'll have you arrested."

"I don't think so," I said nonchalantly as I fished through her roomy bag in search of her cell phone. I found it shortly in the zipper compartment.

"Smile!" I aimed the phone at her and snapped a photo.

She made of face of utter disgust.

I tsk-tsked and shook my head with mock-disdain. "No selfies for you today."

"Shut up and undo me!" she spat back at me.

"What do you think, girls? Does she look pretty in pink?" asked Pussy.

"Very!" Libby, Swell, and I responded in unison.

"Who are you?" Kat hissed, her green eyes flaring at Pussy.

"Someone you're never going to forget. And this is my girlfriend, Swell."

After a succulent kiss, Swell rolled her pierced tongue around her lips and in her husky voice said, "Hi, babe."

"Oh my fucking God," Kat cried out, heaving on the bed and trying desperately to free herself from the restraints that were attached to the brass headboard and footboard.

Pussy snickered. "What do you say, girls? Should we find out how pink the bitch's pussy is?"

"I'd say it's showtime." I handed Libby the phone.

"Lights, camera, action!" shouted Libby, adjusting the phone's camera setting to video while Swell reached for a large pair of scissors on the night table. Starting at the hemline, she began slicing Kat's dress apart, inch by silky inch.

"What the fuck are you doing?" shrieked Kat. "This is a two-thousand-dollar Armani!"

"Well, now, bitch, it's two-thousand-dollar rag." Swell grinned wickedly as she tossed the scissors aside and simply tore apart the rest of the dress with her bare hands. The hiss of the shredding fabric was like music to my ears. In a few harsh breaths, Kat was stripped down to her matching black bra and thong.

Kat's raging eyes met mine. "What's this all about, Jennifer? Is this just some form of revenge for Blake dumping your sorry ass for me?"

Poker-faced, I slipped my hand into my pocket, and in slow motion, I lowered Blake's magnificent snow-flake diamond ring onto my ring finger as she watched with wide-eyed confusion. A giddy smile lit my face.

"News flash, Kat. Blake and I never broke up."

"I don't fucking believe you," she snorted. "He told me this morning it was over between the two of you and that he loves *me*."

I rolled my eyes. "Actually his exact words were: 'Kat, you've always been the one. I love you so fucking much. My cock can't wait to ravish you.'"

Kat's mouth fell open. She looked as if she'd been struck by lightning. She had put two and two together.

My eyes narrowed with fury. "You fucking drugged Blake and made it look like he was seducing you. I bet the evidence is still right here on your phone."

"Give me back my phone, you cunt!"

I smirked. "Can't. My friend Libby needs to use it."

She fired a dirty look at my bestie. Libby aimed the phone at her and said, "Smile."

Kat made a face, her stunning features scrunching with rage.

Click.

"Are we done now?" she grunted.

Crawling onto the bed, Pussy chimed in. "Actually, we haven't yet begun."

In one swift move, she tore off Kat's scanty lace thong while Swell ripped apart her front closure bra and slid it down her arms. A look of terror washed over Kat's face. Her implants quivered. God, they were big!

"What are you going to do to me?" asked Kat, her voice trembling.

Pussy flicked her tongue just above Kat's hairless triangle. "Nothing. Ask me what it's going to look like I'm doing...*Everything!*"

"No!" shrieked Kat, frantically trying to bolt from the bed.

It was futile. Pussy spread Kat's long, toned legs farther apart. Holding down her thighs, she buried her head deep between them. I watched while Libby filmed everything on the bitch's cell phone. Though Pussy wasn't actually licking Kat or doing anything else, she pretended she was. Pussy, the porn star, was just being a great actress.

Kat continued to scream, her body jerking and arching, and her face contorting. Pussy lifted her head and smiled for the camera and then buried her head again between Kat's thighs. Soon her partner got into the act, climbing onto the bed and pretending to be going down Kat's enormous fake boobs. Of course, her mouth never touched down on them, but her moves were effective. Though neither woman was in any way performing any kind of sexual act, Kat was writhing and whimpering. Libby, bless her heart, was filming everything from every angle. I swear, I wouldn't be surprised if she left her research job at Conquest and moved into production. She was clearly enjoying every moment.

A tortured expression washed over Kat's face that could easily be interpreted as tortured pleasure. Ecstasy. I kept my eyes glued on her as Pussy whispered something in her ear.

"Yes!" shrieked Kat. The perfect response to Pussy's inaudible scripted line: "Do you want me to stop?"

Sweat beads clustered on Kat's face and chest as Pussy repositioned herself between her spread-eagled legs. Her ass in the air, the porn star buried her head back into Kat's center, and as she bopped it up and down, she hummed. It looked like she was going down on Kat and bringing her to the edge. What an actress! Libby was still capturing everything, shooting the scene from all the right angles. Just like a pro!

"Please!" cried Kat. "Please, please, please." It just couldn't be more perfect. Kat sounded as if she was begging to come.

After one more "please," Pussy pulled away and Kat let out a giant sigh of relief. Her body went slack.

Yes, yes, yes! With a wag of a finger, I signaled to Libby to stop shooting. We had what we needed. My production classes at USC had really paid off.

"Hope it was as good for you as it was for me," purred Pussy as she climbed off the bed.

Fury flickered in Kat's eyes. "Fuck you. Let me go!"

Pussy smiled smugly. "Not yet."

"My turn," chimed in Swell, her voice as deep as a man's.

Terror washed over Kat's face.

With a wink, Pussy said, "Come on, ladies. Let's go play gin rummy. Hope you know how."

"Gin," I shouted ten minutes later, seated cross-legged around a coffee table in the anteroom. And at that moment, I heard Kat cry out, "stop it," repeatedly. I hoped Swell, who I didn't know before today, wasn't hurting her. Or violating our agreement and sexually assaulting her. As I flipped over my cards, I asked Pussy if she thought everything was all right.

"Chill, honey. Don't you worry. Swell is an artist."

I wanted to believe her. We played several rounds of rummy, and I was thrilled to learn that both Pussy and Swell were coming to the wedding. Before we could re-shuffle the deck yet again, Swell strutted into the room. She greeted us with a wicked twisted grin.

"Everything went smoothly. The slut has something to remember today by. Come see."

Leaving the deck of cards on the table, the three of us followed Swell back to the bedroom. Still bound to the bed, Kat was now blindfolded and screaming. "What the fuck did you to do me, you fucking bull dyke?"

I moved in closer and my eyes popped. At the same time, Libby and I burst into mad laughter. We were laughing so hard we were crying.

"What the fuck are you laughing about? Take off this goddamn blindfold, you bitches."

Swell did as bid. "Oh my fucking god," shrieked Kat upon making eye contact with her chest.

"Some of my finest work ever," boasted Swell.

Inked across Kat's breastbone was one word. Of course, I should have known. With all her tattoos, Pussy's girlfriend Swell was a tattoo artist.

"I was going to ink "BITCH," but this is so much better."

BUTCH. I was laughing so hard I wet my pants.

Kat couldn't stop shrieking. Libby raised Kat's cell phone to take a photo.

"Stop it!" wailed Kat.

Too late. *CLICK.*

"Lib, make sure you e-mail me everything."

My bestie gave me a thumbs up. After my laughter died down, my eyes clashed with Kat's.

"What the fuck do you want?" she seethed.

"It's simple. I want you to leave the country by tomorrow and not come back until Blake and I are married."

"Is that a threat?" Venom poured from her mouth.

"No, it's an ultimatum. If I don't have proof, I'm going to send the footage and photos to your mother. And post it on YouTube and all over Instagram."

"You wouldn't!"

"I would."

Libby chimed in. "And it would be perfect for the new show Blake's developing—*America's Sexiest Home Videos.*

Kat's mouth dropped open, forming a perfect O.

I shot her a wry smile. Oh, and by the way, if one word of your past with Blake leaks out—Which. I. Know. All. About.—you can count on the same."

Kitty-Kat was too shocked to say a word. Her wide-opened mouth remained frozen.

Grinning, Libby handed me Kat's cell phone and I slipped it into a pocket. The four of us pivoted toward the door.

"You're leaving me here?" Kat called out in a panic.

"I'll call security shortly. Enjoy your stay at The Beverly Hills Hotel."

With that, my production staff and I said adieu to my shrieking and cursing nemesis and headed to the Polo Lounge to celebrate a job well done. Our own little wrap party. We couldn't stop laughing.

Two hours and two bottles of champagne later, an e-mail dinged on my phone. It was from Kat, who must have made her way home. No message. Only an attachment. A round-trip ticket to Rio in her name. The date of return was not till January. A triumphant smile lit my face as I put my cell phone away. Fingers crossed Blake and I wouldn't be honeymooning there.

A waiter came by, and I took care of the bill.

Fuck the Bitch was a fait accompli.

Chapter 11

Jennifer

When I told Blake the story of how I took Kat down, he doubled over with laughter. Then, recovered from his drugging, he gave me an epic fucking that for sure belonged in *The Guinness Book of World Records*. I had so many orgasms I lost count.

We couldn't be happier that Kat was out of the picture. But things were no less stressful. In fact, they were more stressful. With the wedding only a month away, Enid was in panic mode. In addition to losing Kat, Jeffrey, the receptionist, quit on her. Little did she know he was starting up his own event planning business and had stolen her list of "preferred" vendors. I knew this from Chaz, who now was dating Jeffrey. It was hot and heavy and I was so happy for him.

I spoke to my mom everyday. Dad was doing great. Except he'd become a little bit of a *kvetch,* complaining constantly about how slowly my mother drove. She begged Blake and me to go to Boise for Thanksgiving, but as much I wanted to, I couldn't. In addition to catching up on my crazy workload (which I was frantically trying to wrap up before the wedding), there were so many last minute wedding details to attend to, including meeting with Blake's rabbi…a wedding cake taste-testing…a meeting with the bandleader to go over our playlist…applying for a marriage license…and going for Monique Hervé's final dress fitting as well as Chaz's first one. Last not but least, there were also all those thank you notes to write. The wedding gifts kept pouring in. The final headcount was at 1150!

On the Saturday after Thanksgiving, which we celebrated at Blake's parents' house, I was going to meet Chaz downtown for my first dress fitting. I couldn't wait to see what he'd designed. He knew the vintage look I wanted but had been very secretive, wanting to surprise me when it was close to finalized. At the crack of dawn, I got a call. With Blake still sound asleep, I reached for my cell phone on the nightstand. It was Chaz.

"Jenny-Poo, it's gone," he said, before I could even say hi. His voice sounded frantic.

I bolted upright to a sitting position. "Chaz, what are you talking about?"

"Your dress. There was a fire in the studio last night. Everything was destroyed."

"Oh my God!" I said the three words so loudly I woke up Blake.

"Baby, what's going on?" he asked groggily.

"Chaz, sweetie, hold on." I turned to Blake and told

him the news. He was almost as devastated as I was. I returned my attention to Chaz.

"Chaz, where are you?"

"I'm here at the studio. You wouldn't believe what it looks like."

"I'll be there in twenty minutes." Chaz, who had always been there for me, needed my moral support. Though Blake insisted on going downtown with me, I told him to stay put. In five minutes, I was dressed and out the door.

Libby and Jeffrey were already at Chaz's studio. Or should I say former studio. We stood in a line like four zombies taking in the damage. It was worse than I'd imagined. In addition to the smut-covered walls and charred bolts of fabric, the fire department had gutted and flooded the loft-like space to put out the fire. The studio was a shell of what it had been with puddles of water everywhere along with exposed wires and beams. And it was still smoking.

"Do they know what caused the fire?" A dark thought crossed my suspicious mind. Did Enid or Monique possibly set it? I wouldn't put it past those two wicked women to do something so evil. Or did Kat have something to do with it from wherever she was to get back at me? That psychopath was capable of anything.

Chaz twisted his lips. "The fire department determined it was definitely due to an electrical short. The wiring in this old building is not up to code."

"That's awful," I murmured, relieved that none of those horrid women had anything to do with it. But it didn't make things any better.

My stinging eyes gravitated to a blackened mannequin in the corner. On it were charred remnants of tulle and lace. The dress was burnt beyond recognition. My heart sunk. My fairy-tale gown had gone up in smoke. It belonged in a morgue.

Chaz followed my gaze. "Oh, Jenny-Poo. It was so beyond."

"Maybe you can make another one," chirped Libby, the optimist, before I could utter a word.

Chaz's shoulders slumped. "I wish, but not a fat chance in hell. I have to find a temporary studio, deal with the insurance company, and then replace all the samples for my upcoming Spring line. Plus, it would take over a month to get the imported fabrics I used. Oh, my Jenny-Poo, I'm so sorry."

Masking my disappointment, I wrapped my arm around Chaz's deflated shoulders. "Chaz, shit happens. The most important thing is you're okay."

Jeffrey clasped my despondent friend's hand. "Honey, I'm going to be there for you. Maybe, I'll do a small fundraiser and invite your top clients and our friends to get things going."

"Count me in." I smiled for the first time, grateful that Chaz finally had a significant other in his life who genuinely loved him. If I ever had to spearhead an event, I knew who was going to be my coordinator.

"And wedding girl, if that bitch Enid gives you any grief, you let me know. I've got plenty of dirt on her and her slutty cohort Monique."

"Oooh, like what?" cooed Chaz, instantly cheered up by juicy gossip.

"They give each other pussy."

My eyes almost popped out of their sockets. "No way. They're gay?"

"Way. Gayer than eight guys blowing nine guys. Enid's husband doesn't know she's a lesbo."

Over breakfast which I treated everyone to, Jeffrey shared more titillating tidbits about Enid and Monique. Enid was a screamer and used a whip. Why should that surprise me? And Monique liked it in her bony butt. We were shrieking and howling at everything Jeffrey revealed—from their feather fetish to their lesbian video fetish. Wow! If I ever had the need to send Enid the video I shot of her daughter she might actually get off on it. I couldn't wait to tell Blake.

December was here in no time. Things for the wedding

were falling into place. The wedding rehearsal—and dinner following at The Bel Air Hotel—were all set up for the night before the monumental event. To my delight, Mrs. Cho's adorable little daughters were going to be my flower girls and walk down the aisle with Marcy's twin sons, the ring bearers. Mom and Dad were flying in that morning. And true to his word, Dad would be walking me down the aisle albeit with a cane.

Gloria Zander gave me a surprise bridal shower. Jeffrey, whose client list was growing rapidly, helped her plan it. Held at Shutters, a chic beachside hotel in Santa Monica, Libby was there along with some of my friends from USC and my rape support group. And guess who else was there—Grandma!—though Blake's mother couldn't make it as she was being honored at some long-standing luncheon for her philanthropic accomplishments. To my delight, Vera Nichols, Blake's sassy Vegas manager, also attended as well as Pussy and Swell. And so did Mrs. Cho. The only person whose presence I sorely missed was my mom; she was afraid to leave Dad alone though he'd insisted she fly out. Libby, God bless her, Skyped her in, so she virtually attended. By the end of the lovely afternoon champagne tea, we were all buzzed, and as Grandma rightly said, "Bubala, you have enough sexy *shmexy* undies for Blakela to tear off to last a lifetime." I was going to start that night.

Later that week, I had my final fitting for

Monique's wedding dress. I'd resigned myself to being the mermaid bride, not the princess bride. Knowing Monique and Enid were secretly having an affair, I could barely keep a straight face as the former made more alterations to my dress. The dress wasn't perfect, but I hoped my wedding would be. Soon, I'd be floating down the aisle. With all the ups and downs I'd been through, my special day couldn't get here soon enough.

The dress had to be taken in. I'd lost some weight from stress. I'd read on some bridal blog this was common, but Blake was worried about me. He felt between the wedding and my work, I was taking on more than I could chew. He was right, but that's just the way I was. I couldn't wait for our honeymoon—which Blake had planned all on his own. He was mum on the destination. I couldn't suck—or fuck—it out of him. All I knew was it some place neither of us had ever been.

There was one other problem—Bradley. Ever since that restaurant incident, he'd e-mailed me constantly. I refused to open his e-mails and simply put them in my trash file and then deleted them permanently. I wanted nothing to do with him, and I never wanted to see him again. I didn't tell Blake about the e-mails. For all intents and purposes, Bradley Wick, DDS, was dead to me.

On the Tuesday of the week before my wedding, I had my last support group meeting of the year. I wasn't feeling well. All day long, I'd been experiencing cramping. For sure, stress. Blake didn't want me to go. Not only because of my rundown state, but because there had been a recent chain of gang-driven crimes in the Venice Beach neighborhood where we met. But I insisted. We were going to have a small Christmas party with a gift exchange. Plus, I wanted to thank Dr. Williams for her kindness as well as hug my friends who'd shared and learned to face their fears like me. Blake wasn't thrilled, to put things mildly. He still had to learn I was a big girl and could take care of myself. And he couldn't always control me.

The meeting lasted about an hour. Instead of our normal routine of taking turns to talk about our rape-related issues, we feasted on eggnog and snacks we'd each brought along and shared what we were doing over the holidays. Dr. Williams and my sweet fellow rape victims had been invited to the wedding and were all looking forward to attending. Before leaving, Dr. Williams and I exchanged a hug. She'd helped me so much—especially with my trust issues. I was grateful Blake had urged me to join the group after the Springer attack.

The mid December air was chilly, especially for LA. Wearing only a lightweight wool sweater, I hugged myself as I walked quickly to my car which was parked a few blocks away. The poorly lit streets were dark and desolate. Nearby sirens sounded in my ears. And then I heard footsteps. So I thought. I anxiously looked over my shoulder. No one. My weary, distrustful mind was playing tricks on me. Paranoia was a recurring feeling among rape victims. We feared being followed and thought it could happen again. Holding my car keys, I picked up my pace until I reached my vehicle. Before I could unlock the door, a harsh voice called out my name.

Startled, I flipped around and accidentally dropped my keys. I bent down to retrieve them, but another hand got to them first.

Chapter 12

Blake

As much as I loved my tiger, she still knew how to piss me off. She could be as stubborn as a mule. I didn't want her to go to her rape support group. She was overworked and rundown. Plus, knowing there had been a bunch of gang-related incidents in the seedy Venice Beach neighborhood where they met bugged the shit out of me. If something happened to my tiger, I'd just about die. I'd almost lost her once; I couldn't lose her again. It wouldn't have killed her not to go, but it would kill me if something bad happened to her. I was as protective of her as I was possessive.

Despite my protestations, she insisted on going and told me to take a chill pill. There was nothing I could do to stop her—except tie her up and hold her down—which, in retrospect, I should have done. My cock twitched at the image of her all tied up in ropes. It made me horny as hell. Later when she got home, I was going to live out this fantasy and give her a fucking she wouldn't forget.

She'd left the office early to head over to her group,

which met weekly at seven p.m. At 7:30, I packed up my briefcase and headed to my car. Once settled inside, I flipped on the radio. Breaking news. The body of a badly beaten young woman had been discovered in Venice, close to Jennifer's support group center. Her wallet had been stolen and her identity was still unknown. Police and paramedics had rushed to the scene of the crime and were still there. My heart leapt into my throat. I yanked my stick shift into first gear and peeled out of the parking lot.

Fuck. Fuck. FUCK.

Chapter 13

Jennifer

Crouching, my unexpected companion and I were face to face. His nostrils flared. My pulse sounded in my ears.

"Bradley, what are you doing here? And what do you want?"

One word: "You." His fetid breath assaulted me. Shit. He was uncharacteristically drunk.

I tensed but tried to remain calm and thought I could reason with him. But before I could get my lips to move, he shoved me against the car. My head banged against the frame, and in a painful breath, his slimy lips were all over mine and his hands were groping my breasts. The words "Stop it" stayed lodged in my throat as I tried to fight him off. Tearing at his thinning hair. Pushing him away. He bit my lip with his monstrous teeth and I could taste blood in my mouth. *His balls! Go for his balls!* But before I could reach for them, he grabbed my wrists tightly.

"Fuck you, Jennifer," he hissed.

"No. Fuck you, you bastard." Another voice. A

voice I recognized.

In a split second, Bradley was off me. Dangling by his collar in the hands of the man I loved. Blake! My hero!

Burning with rage, Blake set Bradley on his feet, spun him around, and—POW!—punched him hard in the face. Wincing, Bradley staggered against the car. Blood poured from his nose. Wiping my own bloody lip, I crawled away and stood up. My heart pounded as I watched Blake punch him again. Bradley moaned loudly and put his small hand to his bloody face.

Blake lifted his hand once more, his fingers balled into a tight fist. Bradley turned his head away and cowered.

"Man, don't hit me again!" My despicable ex was practically sobbing.

A sudden rush of fear surged inside me. Blake was capable of murder. He had killed for me once and he could do it again. As much as I despised Bradley, I couldn't let that happen.

"Please, Blake," I pleaded. "Leave him alone! He's had enough."

Without acknowledging me, Blake held Bradley fastened in his fiery gaze. My heart galloped and my throat clenched. To my relief, he lowered his fist and then slapped both hands on Bradley's shoulders, shoving him against my car door. Bradley's blood-stained lips quivered.

"Let me go," he whimpered.

Blake's lips snarled. "Don't you *ever* mess with my girl. She's mine now. You fuck with her, you fuck with me."

Bradley trembled.

"Trust me. You'll be asking Santa for your two front teeth."

Bradley parted his lips as if wanted to say something. Blake stopped him.

"And if I ever see you touch her, I'll cut off your little dick. You'll be sucking thumbkin."

I watched as Blake kicked him square in the balls. Groping his groin, Bradley groaned and crumpled to the ground. Blake spat at him.

"Now get the hell out of here, Dickwick. I never want to see you again."

I watched as Bradley crawled away.

Blake's rage didn't die down. With pounding steps, he moved my way. I gazed up at him. His razor-sharp eyes pierced me as he held me fierce in his gaze.

"What the fuck was he doing here?"

"Oh, Blake! He must have followed me. He's been stalking me online."

"Screw 'Oh Blake.'" A rage that frightened me swept over Blake's face. "Why the hell didn't you tell me?"

I shriveled against the hood of the car. "You've been away. Busy. Preoccupied." I stuttered every word.

"Fuck you, Jennifer."

I shuddered at his angry words.

"You didn't listen to me. I had a bad feeling about tonight. I told you I didn't want you to come here, but you did."

"But—"

He cut me off. "Fuck 'but.' You need to be punished."

He'd punished me once before. But it was playful. I'd screwed up pancakes and he'd fucked me on the kitchen floor, dousing me with maple syrup. But this was different. There was an intensity to him now I'd never known before. It both frightened and excited me.

He flipped me around so I was bent over the hood. My hands splayed on the cold metal. The headlights pressed against my middle. My head was bowed down, but I could still see his enraged reflection in the windshield. "Blake, what are you going to do to me?"

"I'm going to fuck some sense into you."

A retribution fuck. I was strangely aroused. "Fuck you, Blake."

"Fuck you, tiger," he growled, shoving down my skirt along with my panties in one swift swoop and then spreading my legs apart.

His giant cock needed no warm-up. And apparently, my pussy wasn't going to get one either. With a loud carnal grunt, he thrust his thick length into me. And began to ram me. This was fucking with no mercy. I winced. He slapped my ass. I winced again. Hot, salty tears sprinkled my cheeks. He pounded harder, digging his nails into my hips. I rocked into him, oddly enjoying every erotic minute.

"Blake, why are you doing this to me?"

"Because. *Thrust.* I. *Thrust.* Love. *Thrust.* You."

"Don't you have a better way of expressing yourself?" I blissfully wept the words.

In response to my question, an arm wrapped around my waist and I could feel his fingertips trail down to my soaking wet center. He began to rub my clit fervently while he continued to pummel me. Shrieks escaped from my lungs as an orgasm spiraled inside me, taking every cell with it. But before I could climax, he pulled his hand away, leaving my hot bundle of nerves bereft.

"Blake, please," I pleaded. "I need to come."

"I need an apology."

"Anything." I was desperate.

"Say you're sorry."

"Sorry."

"And that you'll never disobey me."

"Never." *Nonsense.*

"Good." To my relief, his hand returned to my clit, and he circled away. My orgasm resumed as if there had never been an intermission. It was coming at me at full force. Crashing through me. "Oh, Blake," I screamed out as his own powerful climax met mine. A head-on collision. No pun intended.

"Tiger," he groaned, pulling me back against him as his hot release coated my thighs.

I felt him pull out and then he flipped me around. A mixture of madness and passion flickered in his half-mast blue eyes. They held me prisoner as he cradled my face in his large hands. Tenderness replaced the fury.

"Are you okay?" His voice was soft.

I nodded. His unblinking eyes bore into me.

"Tiger, I almost lost you once. I can't lose you again. If you die, I die. You own my heart."

My lips quivered at his powerful words. Lifting one of my hands, he slipped it under his suit jacket and held it against his heart. I could feel it beating against my palm. I gazed up at his beautiful face. "Blake, one more promise. I'm never going to leave you."

"Thank you baby. I needed to hear that." He held me close to him, as if never wanting to let me go.

Chapter 14

Blake

We headed home in one car. Mine. I told Jen to leave hers in Venice. She protested, but I told her I'd have someone from the office pick it up in the morning. And if one of the local gangs vandalized or jacked it, I didn't give a shit. I'd buy her a new car. And it wasn't going to be another Kia.

We drove in silence. Her hand stayed clutched on my hand gripping the shift. Sam Smith's "Stay with Me" played on the radio. The words of this soulful singer's song resonated deep inside me. How close I had come to losing my tiger. One time after another. I didn't want to think about it. I just knew I couldn't live without her.

When we got to our condo, I valeted the car and led her through the lobby, my arm wrapped around her shoulders. We were almost one.

Once inside the apartment, I drew a hot bath. The rope fantasy I'd had earlier in the day had gone down the drain. It just didn't make sense now. Right now, I just needed to hold my tiger. Let her know she was mine. Make up for punishing her. And rid myself of guilt. I felt bad about my angry fuck, yet she'd seemed turned on, not offended.

After peeling off her clothes, which I intended to burn since Dickwick had touched them, I helped her into the tub. My tub was luxurious. Big enough to let six foot three me stretch out, and it had a Jacuzzi. Truthfully, due to our hectic work schedules, Jen and I hadn't enjoyed it much. Mostly, we took showers together.

I watched as she sunk into the breast-deep water. Her sigh was like a symphony to my ears. Turning on the Jacuzzi, I shrugged off my clothes and joined her, settling behind her. She was in my arms, her slender body and head resting against my chest and shoulders. The water gurgled around us, the bubbling jets caressing and massaging. We were in a zone.

I grabbed a large sponge, squirted some liquid soap on it, and then began to wash her everywhere. Dickwick needed to be erased.

"I'm sorry about tonight," I breathed against her delicate neck as I washed the back of it and her shoulders. "Did I hurt you?"

She arched against me, splaying her hands on my thighs under the water.

"No, Blake. You can never hurt me."

I pondered her soft words. They were true. I wasn't capable of hurting my tiger. My burning desire to protect her and fear of losing her ruled me. I'd never thought about the consequences of my actions with any woman. She made me feel things—emotions—I'd never experienced. And sometimes go to extremes. Kill for her if I had to. I wanted to be her superhero forever.

Silently, I continued to sponge her. She hummed into the percussion of the bubbles. As I soaped her tender tits, her chest rose and fell against me. My cock rose beneath her. Her half-wet ponytail tickled me. Impulsively, I pulled it loose from its elastic band and it free fell, cascading over her shoulders like a velvet cape. The silkiness grazed my chest.

Keeping one hand cupped on her pert rosebud-tipped tit, I reached for the tube of shampoo. The only one she used. Gloria's Secret Very Cherry Vanilla. I squeezed a few dollops onto her hair and, with both hands, began massaging it into her scalp until there was a rich lather. The erotic squishy sound and intoxicating scent aroused me, my cock and heart swelling with love and lust, one physically, the other emotionally. I had to have her. Not fuck her. But make love to her. She was thinking the same thing.

"Oh, Blake," she said dreamily. "Take me. Make love to me."

Gently, I lifted her hips onto my erection. She lowered herself onto my thick, aching length, taking me all the way. God, she felt good. So fucking good. I squeezed my eyes shut and let her know with a moan.

On the next heated breath, I was gliding in and out of her, my mouth showering her with kisses everywhere it could, my hands working her slick clit, the water bubbling with love. We came passionately together.

Oh baby, stay with me. You're all I need.

Chapter 15

Jennifer

Time flew by. The weekend of our wedding was here before I knew it.

On Friday, December nineteenth, the day of the rehearsal, the familiar ring of my cell phone jolted me out of my sleep. I hadn't slept well at all. The last minute wedding details had vexed me, and both my mind and my stomach were aflutter. I was wound up as tight as a ball of yarn but could unravel at any minute. Moreover, I was sure I was getting my damn period. I'd been cramping on and off all week and the littlest thing made me cry.

The smell of fresh coffee wafted in the air. Blake was already up and out of bed, for sure in the kitchen. I glanced at the clock on my nightstand. It was seven a.m. The phone rang again and I stretched my arm to reach for it. With half-closed eyes, I registered who was calling. It was my mom. Of course, I had told her to call me when they were about to take off. My parents would be here in two hours. In plenty of time for the rehearsal and dinner tonight. I'd wanted them to come out earlier in the week, but unfortunately, Dad couldn't forego his final, much-needed therapy sessions—especially since he was bent on walking me down the aisle.

My mother's teary-eyed voice sounded before I could even say hi. "Jennifer, honey, I have terrible news."

My heart leapt into my throat and I bolted upright. An inner panic button went off. Had something happened to my father? "Is Dad okay?" I choked out.

"Honey, he's fine. But our flight has been canceled."

"Mom, what do you mean?" My words were rushed and pitchy.

"It's blizzarding."

"Oh my God. What about a later flight?"

"I'm not sure." My mother's voice wavered. "According to airport officials, the storm is expected to get worse."

Tears pricked my eyes, and I could feel a knot in the pit of my stomach. How could this be happening? As a tear escaped, Blake, in just his pajama bottoms, strode into the room, holding two steaming mugs of coffee. He caught a glimpse of me and rushed to my side.

"Jen, what's the matter?" He sat down on the edge of the bed, handing me one of the mugs. It shook in my hand.

"Mom, hold on." Setting the mug on the nightstand, I told Blake what was going on.

Tilting his head back, he huffed a breath. "Jeez. Just what we don't need." My eyes stayed riveted on him as he scooted across the mattress to retrieve his cell phone on the other night table.

"Blake, what are you doing?" I snapped, my nerves getting to me.

"I'm going to see if we can send my father's private plane or the company jet to get them."

Oh, my Blake! I relayed this news to my mom as I listened intently with my other ear to the conversation Blake was having with someone who must be from the Conquest travel department. His eyebrows were knitted as he went back and forth with them.

"Fuck." He flung the phone on the bed. My heart sunk deeper. I knew it was not good. His eyes met mine.

"Jen, they're closing the airport. No planes are allowed to depart or land."

Shit. It was even worse than I thought. With a lump in my throat, I shared the bad news with my mom. Tearfully, she told me she was going to ask Father Murphy, who was with them, to pray. As I was about to say good-bye, my dad got on the phone. Tears of my own were now streaming down my cheeks.

"Hi, Dad," I sniffled as Blake massaged my shoulders.

"Jennifer Leigh McCoy, you stop crying right now. Your mother and I may not be there tonight for the rehearsal, but we will be there tomorrow for your wedding. I said I was going to walk my little girl down the aisle, and I never break my promises."

No, he never had broken a promise in all my life. I wiped my eyes. With a final sniffle and an ounce of optimism, I told my darling dad I believed him and how much I loved him. My love for him, like for Blake, was immeasurable.

Blake went into the office for a few hours while I took the day off. I still had a million details to attend to, plus Enid had insisted I get my hair, nails, and makeup done for tonight's events. And a facial. Soon after Blake departed, I canceled all my appointments. The day was gloomy—for the first time in a long time, gray and overcast. Mirroring exactly how I felt. Mom and Dad had gone back home, and all my googling made me feel worse. The blizzard could last up to twenty-four hours. And it was spreading across the Midwest. Despite my father's promise, the reality that my parents might miss my wedding was eating away at me. And on top of all my worries, I felt like pure crap. More than just tension. Shooting pains stabbed my gut. I was beginning to worry if it was something beyond nerves and the onset of my period. Was I getting sick?

Blake returned mid afternoon. His sultry voice

awoke me; I'd dozed off.

"Jen, it's almost four o'clock. You should start getting ready."

As I fluttered my eyes open and sat up, another one of those sharp pangs dug into me. Clutching my stomach and grimacing, I let out a soft moan, but not soft enough to be unnoticed by Blake. He dashed to my side.

"Are you okay, baby?" His voice was thick with concern.

"Blake, I think I might be coming down with something." It was that time of year the flu was rampant. Many co-workers had come down with it, along with Blake's college roommate, Jake, who was not going to make it to the rehearsal or wedding. Even though I'd had a flu shot, it didn't make me immune.

"Are you sure?" My soon-to-be husband tenderly kissed my forehead. "You don't seem to have a fever."

Well, that was good news. Maybe it *was* just nerves.

"C'mon. Let's take a shower together and get ready."

Maybe a shower was just what I needed.

Wrong. We fucked. I felt worse.

The rehearsal at Blake's parents' house started at six. I was wearing the stunning ivory dress Blake surprised me with in Paris along with my mother's lovely cashmere birthday sweater while Blake was dressed in one of his sexy tapered dark suits. He looked dashing. I, to be honest, still looked—and felt—like crap. Even the makeup I'd applied, including the little extra blush and eye shadow, couldn't camouflage my pallor or glazed eyes.

We got there a little early. Mayhem. Pure mayhem. That's the only way to describe the scene. It was like a movie production. Except crazier and more chaotic. Workers were everywhere, and amidst them was a frazzled Enid, dressed to the nines, heels and all, shouting orders through a megaphone. Hundreds of white folding chairs were being set up in the Bernsteins' vast backyard for tomorrow's ceremony, and a giant tent was in the process of being erected for the reception.

"Goddammit. How hard is it to fill a bowl of water and stick a stupid fish in it?" Enid screamed into a walkie talkie. And then into her ringing cell phone, "What do you mean, you idiot? I asked for Beluga caviar, not Sevruga. Just deliver it, but after tomorrow, you're fired."

"Oh, hello Jennifer," she said in a most condescending tone upon taking note of me. She snubbed Blake, who had his arm wrapped around me. I told her my parents wouldn't be coming to the rehearsal because of a snowstorm.

She rolled her eyes and let out a haughty huff of air. And then she narrowed her eyes at Blake. "Seriously, Blake, this would have never happened if you'd married Katrina."

Though she was a continent away, the mention of her name made my skin prickle. Blake held his own.

"*Seriously*, Enid, you need to get your head examined. You're one sick bitch."

Like mother like daughter. Enid's jaw dropped to the floor and stayed there while Blake ushered me away to mingle with our guests.

Seeing friends and family was a welcomed comfort.

Overlooking the backyard, the elegant, spacious veranda began to fill with all the wedding party participants—from the eight hired blond bimbo bridesmaids from Central Casting to those near and dear to us.

Blake's sister Marcy, upon arriving, gave me a hug and then observed me in true doctorly fashion.

"Jennifer, are you all right? You look very pale."

"Yes. Just a case of pre-wedding nerves," I said as another gut-wrenching pang stabbed me. The good actress I was, I smiled through the pain. Perceptive Libby shot me a concerned look. Her sharp, analytical mind could cut through bullshit like a knife.

Enid's thundering voice intercepted my thoughts. She held her megaphone to her face. "Attention, everyone. The rehearsal is about to begin."

One by one, Enid gave the wedding party their marching orders as if she were General Patton. With Rabbi Silverstein already at the altar, Grandma led off the procession. She was followed by the groomsmen, who proceeded in pairs and included Chaz and Jeffrey, and then by Blake's best man, Jaime. With a squeeze of my hand, Blake was the next to go. His parents flanked him. As he stepped onto the verdant lawn, Blake looked over his shoulder and blew me a kiss. For a fleeting moment, my gloom lifted. I blew one back at him.

As he disappeared into the ominous night, the bevy of bridesmaids, which included Gloria and Marcy, trailed behind him.

Libby and I were the only ones left. Along with Marcy's twin boys, the ring bearers, and Mrs. Cho's daughters, the flower girls. They had managed to score a snow globe and, huddled on the floor in the corner, were watching the little fish inside it swim around in circles. Squeals and laughter filled the air.

"Children," barked Enid. "Your turn. Chop chop!"

The children ignored her. They were too busy playing.

Scowling, Enid marched over to them. She snatched the snow globe and, to my wide-eyed horror, tossed it across the room. The glass shattered and the fish went flying.

Mrs. Cho's sweet little girls burst into tears.

"Meanie!" cried out one of the twins.

My eyes traveled to the fish flapping madly on the floor by my feet. In my overcharged emotional state, tears seared my eyes. The poor little thing. He was gasping for air. I could feel his pain. At this very moment, I, too, felt like a fish out of water. Helpless. Suffocating. Desperate. I fell to my knees and scooped the tiny orange creature into my palms. In a heartbeat, Libby, wearing one of Chaz's little black dresses, was by my side with a bowl of water. *My Libby! Always there for me!*

"Get up, you ridiculous girls," seethed Enid as I struggled to get the fish into the bowl. He was squirming and jumping in my cupped hands. The captivated children had gathered around us.

Libby's freckles jumped off her face as they did when she was enraged. She cranked her neck and gazed up at Enid.

"Shut up, you bitch!" she barked as I finally managed to get the fish safely into the water. It happily swam about.

The cheering children burst out in laughter. "She said the b-word," singsonged one of the twins.

Enid was livid, but for the first time all day, I was on the brink of laughter. Libby didn't hold back and high-fived one of the twins.

"Move it, you imps," growled Enid, snapping her bony fingers at the children, "or I'm going to replace you with some *professional* children who know how to behave."

One of Mrs. Cho's daughters stuck her tongue out at the bitch while the other flung a handful of seashells at her from the basket she was holding.

"You little brats!" Enid screeched as she broke into a hot flash and began fanning herself. As the flustered wedding planner physically ushered the rambunctious children outside, a clap of thunder resounded.

Shit. Was it going to rain?

Still squatting, Libby gave me a hug. "I love you, Jen. Are you okay?"

I nodded, biting back the urge to tell her the truth.

"Next!" shouted Enid.

"That's me." With an affectionate squeeze of my hand, my maid of honor stood up and filed out the door. *Don't leave me, Lib!*

I was all alone. I should have been happy. Excited. But unbearable sadness devoured me along with agonizing pain.

Mendelssohn's "Bridal March" drifted into my ear. My cue.

"Go!" screamed Enid with a sweeping wave of her free hand.

Slowly rising to my feet, I slumped toward the door, so missing my father and my mom. As I stepped outside, a bolt of lightning flashed and then midway down my lonely, painful walk down the aisle, the sky opened up. A sudden torrent of rain began to pour. In the near distance, the shrieking members of my wedding procession scurried about, dashing into the reception tent for shelter. I heard Enid scream through her megaphone, "Goddamnit. Will someone get me an umbrella?"

I stood there motionless. Tears mingled with the pounding raindrops. They stung my eyes, my skin, and soaked me soul-deep. Ahead of me, one person stood as still as me, drenched under a canopy of drowning flowers. *That* man who was waiting for me. *That* man who would always be there for me, whatever storm we weathered. Somehow, some way, through the tears, the pain, and all the rain, I made my way into his arms.

Chapter 16

Jennifer

"Baby, how do you feel?"

Upon a kiss on my forehead, I peeled my eyes open. One at a time…slowly. Blake came into focus. Consciousness crept through my veins.

This was my day. My special day. But nothing spoke to the moment.

"Like shit," I croaked. I was definitely coming down with a bad flu. I ached all over and last night I'd had the chills. Even Blake's warm body blanketed around me hadn't stopped my teeth from chattering. The rain had only made things worse. Thank goodness, the rehearsal dinner was canceled on account of everyone getting so drenched.

"Fuck," mumbled Blake, grabbing his cell phone. "I'm calling Dr. Klein to find out if there's anything you can take."

I listened as Blake spoke to his family doctor. Pacing, he wanted to know if there was a prescription that would alleviate the symptoms. His mouth twisted as he said in a glum tone, "Okay doctor, I understand. I will."

My heavy-lidded eyes searched his. He shook his head with dismay. "Tiger, there's nothing you can do except take Advil. The doctor said it's likely the new strain of the flu that's becoming epidemic."

"Blake, I don't want you to kiss me after we say our 'I do's.'"

"Baby, I'd kiss you if you had the fucking plague. And I'll carry you down the aisle if I have to."

To prove it, he crushed his lips on my mine. My cell phone rang. I broke the kiss. My heart jumped. It was my mother. I perked up and sighed with relief. Great news! The blizzard had stopped and the airport had re-opened. They were on a flight. She and Dad along with Father Murphy would be here by early afternoon. I suddenly felt much better.

The day was overcast, but at least it had stopped raining. That my parents would be here for my wedding was my ray of sunshine. In slo mo, I threw on some jeans and headed over with Blake to his parents' house at noon. I was carrying a small bag containing white satin heels I'd found at Target and a few bare necessities while Blake had his tux in a garment bag folded over his arm. Despite how crappy I felt, I couldn't wait to see him in it.

Blake's mother, Helen, met us at the front door.

Wearing designer workout clothes, she gave us each a double cheek kiss, careful not to muss her still wet manicured nails. Her coral nail polish perfectly matched the gown she would be wearing.

"Children, you must see what Enid has done," she said excitedly, looping her arm through Blake's and leading us to the sprawling backyard. Holding Blake's other hand, I shared the good news that my parents would be in LA shortly.

"Darling, I'm so thrilled they'll be here," responded Helen as we made our way past the pool. "What do you think?"

Speechless, I couldn't believe my eyes. In the free-form pool with its grotto waterfall, synchronized swimmers from the U.S. Olympic team were practicing their routine while caterers were setting up pre-wedding cocktail stations all around it.

"It's going to be so divine," gushed Helen as she ushered us to the grassy ceremony area.

My eyes popped. The humongous yard had been totally transformed, and not for a minute would one think it had been subject to a downpour. All the white folding chairs were set up, and giant conch shells filled with abundant white roses and blue orchids lined the aisle. Ahead of me, workers were frantically replacing flowers and seashells on the canopy under which Blake and I had kissed in the rain last night. They were also setting up the altar.

"Everything looks beautiful, Mom," Blake muttered, squeezing my clammy hand.

"Oh, darling, the best is yet to come. Wait until you see inside the tent!"

Five minutes later, we were in the throes of the most dazzling spectacle I'd ever seen.

"Wow," I murmured as Helen walked us through it. The vast tent was draped with swags of coral silk and pearl-white tulle. Grandiose chandeliers dripping with strings of pearls and crystal starfish dangled from the soaring ceiling. There must have been close to one hundred tables, still be setting up by frantic workers. Tall crystal vases filled with most amazing white flowers, seashells, pearls, and more of those sparkling starfish adorned each one. And at each seat was a snow globe filled with water, sparkles, and a colorful live fish. The décor was simply breathtaking.

"Come take a look-see at the dance floor, children." With unbounded enthusiasm, Helen led the way and beamed. "Honestly, have you ever seen anything like it?"

I couldn't help but gasp. As if Enid hadn't taken the under-the-sea theme to the extreme, the see-through dance floor was an aquarium filled with colorful tropical fish. I actually felt seasick stepping on it. Or maybe it was more of the flu. Swaying on my feet, I gripped Blake's hand tighter as nausea rose to my chest and another shooting pain ripped through me.

"Are you all right, darling?" asked Helen, lifting a brow as far as she could.

Blake responded before I could. "Jen's feeling a little under the weather. She may have the flu."

"Oh, dear."

"Helen, I just need to rest for a bit. I'm sure I'll be okay." I was lying through my teeth. Despite the Advil, I was feeling worse and worse. The stomach pains had intensified and my energy was depleting.

Blake's mother affectionately clasped my hands in hers. "Of course, darling. You can lie down in one of our guestrooms."

"You will do nothing of the sort!" came a shrill voice. Enid. Dressed in a shrimp-pink silk suit, she stampeded our way. She glanced down at her diamond watch. "You're late. You were supposed to be here at 11:30. Hair and makeup have been waiting patiently for you. And the *In-Style* photographer who's going to document your bridal journey as well as the portrait photographer have been driving me crazy wanting to know where you are. And you've also kept Monique waiting."

Before I could get my mouth to move, an accented voice came through the walkie talkie she was clutching. "*Señora, tenemos un problema. Los peces se están muriendo.* I could actually see steam coming out of Enid's flaring nostrils. "What do you mean the fish are dying? Feed them, you moron, and get someone to go to the fish supply store to buy new ones!"

The image of dead, bloated goldfish floating upside down sickened me further. Suddenly, I just wanted my mom to be with me. And then it hit me. Something was missing. I glared at Enid.

"Enid, where are the place cards my mother shipped?" They weren't on the tables.

She gritted her teeth. "You mean those *quaint* little picture frames with the glued on shells?"

My blood boiled. "Yes."

She snorted. "They'll be on tables at the entrance so our guests will know where they're sitting."

Helen chimed in. "With all due respect for your mother, I insisted we use them. They're really quite charming."

I breathed a sigh of relief and was thankful for Helen's support. I was sure our guests would love them. They were a perfect keepsake. And they would sure last a lot longer than these holed-up, oxygen-deprived goldfish. Maybe a lifetime.

My cell phone rang. I hastily retrieved it from my purse and my spirits brightened. It was my mother. That meant they had landed!

"Mom, you're here?" I said with bated breath.

As her voice filtered into my ears, my heart sunk like the Titanic. "Oh, no!" This just couldn't be happening. Shell-shocked and shaken, I listlessly slipped the phone back into my bag.

"Baby, what's the matter?" Blake was alarmed.

"It's my parents. Their plane was diverted. They're in Dallas along with Father Murphy. They're on a connecting flight, but it won't be here until nine tonight." I fought hard to hold back tears as the conversation ping-ponged back and forth.

Enid: "Darling, let's worry about that problem later."

Helen: "Enid, Jennifer doesn't feel well and this is serious."

Enid: "Puh-lease."

Blake: "Mom, I'm going back to the house to see if we can send Dad's plane to get them."

Helen: "Sweetheart, that's just what I was thinking. If I recall, Dallas by air is three hours away. That means, potentially we can get the McCoys here by five o'clock with the two hour time difference if there aren't any delays. Blake, I'll head back to the house with you."

Helen turned to me and then did something I so needed. She gave me a warm motherly hug. "Darling, keep your chin up. We'll get your parents and Father Murphy here."

I quirked a small, grateful smile. For the first time since I'd known her, I felt a connection to Blake's mother. She had my back.

"Come, now," hissed Enid, wrenching me away. "Let's get down to business."

A violent spasm rocked my abdomen as she hauled me away.

"Finally!" snapped Monique as I staggered into an opulent guest suite on the main floor of the Bernsteins' palatial mansion. Like the rest of their house, it was filled with expensive antiques and artwork. My dress, on a padded hanger, hung from an ornate tri-fold corner mirror while the starfish headpiece was perched on a nearby velvet chaise. Both were wrapped in protective plastic.

Monique was not alone. Two clone-like assistants flanked her and scuttling about was a hip-looking couple who I assumed was doing my hair and makeup.

"Should I change into the dress?" I asked Enid. My voice was weary when it should have been bubbling with excitement. Besides feeling terribly fluish, I was so stressed over my parents.

Enid rolled her eyes at me again. "Of course not. You need to do hair and makeup first. Go to the guest bathroom where you'll find a robe. Get undressed, but be sure to put on your bridal undergarments. And one more thing…please take off that *hideous* jewelry you're wearing. It doesn't go with your dress."

She was referring to the pink tourmaline pendant necklace and matching earrings Blake had given me.

Anger surged inside me. No way. They were staying.

"I'm not taking them off," I said defiantly.

Enid pursed her lips in disgust. "Fine. We'll just photoshop them out for the publicity pictures. Maybe replace them with pearls."

Seething, I bit my tongue as she pointed to the door of the ensuite bathroom. Five minutes later, I emerged wearing a fluffy terrycloth robe and matching slippers. Beneath the robe, I had on the beautiful lace lingerie and silk stockings Gloria had given me at my bridal shower. Clutching my cell phone, I placed the bag with my shoes by one of the couches. Just as hair and makeup were about to begin, my phone rang. Blake! My heart galloping, I hit answer. YES! Great news! His father's private jet would be leaving soon to pick up my parents and Father Murphy. Enid shot me a dirty look as I let Blake know how much I loved him.

"Monique and I will be back shortly. I'm leaving you in very good hands. Philippe and Irma have done hair and makeup for countless celebrities."

My eyes stayed fixed on Enid and my dress designer as they strolled out of the room. I wondered—were they going to get in a little pussy time somewhere? If only Helen knew. Feeling so much more relaxed now knowing my parents would be here in time for my wedding, I inwardly chuckled at the thought.

Seated in a richly upholstered armchair, I told Philippe I wanted my makeup to be as natural as possible (the way Blake preferred it) while Irma worked on my hair. "Ow," I yelped as she yanked it up into a high ponytail.

"What are you putting on my eyes?" I asked Philippe.

"False eyelashes. Your eyes will photograph so much better."

What? I didn't need false lashes. My lashes were long and thick, one of my best features. I fluttered my heavy lids, getting used to the sensation.

One agonizing hour later, he handed me a large hand-mirror. "You look divine," he cooed.

"So divine," echoed Irma, now done with my updo.

Anxiously, I raised the mirror to my face. Gasp! I didn't recognize myself. My lips were painted lobster red; glittery aqua marine eye shadow coated my lids; my lashes looked like fish fins, and my hairstyle resembled an octopus. This was so not me. I looked like a sea monster!

Before I could utter a word, Enid and Monique came breezing back. Enid's suit jacket was unbuttoned and stray hairs fell onto her face. For sure, they'd had a little romp.

"Marvelous," breathed Enid in her throaty voice as she circled me.

"But—"

Her face tightened. "Remember, Jennifer, there are no buts." She turned to Monique. "*Darling,* what do you think?

"Positively sublime. She's so going to be the siren bride. Time to get her into her dress."

I watched as Monique gathered the gown and carefully lifted off the plastic. Ten minutes later, with the helping hands of her assistants, I was in it and wearing my white satin heels along with the glittery starfish headpiece.

I glared at my reflection in the three-way mirror. The bride was supposed to look radiant, but I was anything but. My glazed, heavily made-up eyes blinked back tears. Despite the alterations, the ruffly mermaid-style dress still fit all wrong and the butt pad made me look distorted.

I was swimming in my dress.

I was drowning in a sea of sorrow.

I was floundering for words.

Monique screwed up her face. "How dare you lose more weight! My assistants are going to have to make some last minute alterations."

Enid growled. "I'm going to charge Helen extra for all the unnecessary work and stress you've caused us."

And what about all the stress she'd caused me? I held back treacherous tears as Monique's clones began to pin the *vomiticious* creation down the sides. I so wanted my mom.

Back in my robe, I stumbled to a couch and sat down hunched over. One hand cupped my head, the other my tummy. While Enid excused herself to check on what was going on outside, Monique watched over her assistants as they worked together to stitch down the gown with the portable sewing machine they'd brought along. My cell phone rang. My heart pounding, I slipped it out of the robe pocket. Blake again. More great news! His dad's private plane had landed in Dallas and my parents were on their way. He promised to keep me posted.

"How are you feeling?" he asked, after sharing the good news.

The truth: Like crap. Though my case of nerves had subsided, the shooting pains in my abdomen were coming at me more frequently and sharply. Clutching my stomach, I lied through my teeth and told Blake I was feeling a little better. He didn't need more stress.

"Baby, hang in there. I can't wait to say 'I do'," he breathed into the phone.

"The same. I love you." He returned the words and ended the call as another bolt of pain shot through me. While most brides probably wanted their wedding day to last forever, I couldn't wait for mine to be over. Anxiously, I fiddled with my glittering snowflake diamond ring. The memory of Blake surprising me with it—hidden in a snow globe no less—danced in my head and temporarily took my mind off all my troubles.

A familiar voice cut into the fond memory and widened the small smile on my face. Grandma!

"Bubala, I heard you're coming down *vith* something. Flu *shmu!* I brought you a *bissel* of my chicken soup. Jewish penicillin."

"Enid's going to get mad you're here."

"Enid *shmenid.*" Handing me a steaming bowl of her aromatic soup, she plopped down next to me on the velvet couch. "Eat!" she commanded.

"Thanks, Grandma," I murmured, forcing myself to put a tablespoon of the hot broth to my lips. I blew on it and then sipped the flavorful liquid. You know what? The soup *was* magical. As it coursed through me, I felt a little better. I helped myself to several tablespoons more.

"Mmmm. So good. I'll never make it as good as you."

Grandma flicked her wrist dismissively. "Bubala, you'll learn."

"What the hell are you doing?" Enid. She was back. At the sound of her shrill voice, I almost choked on a mouthful of soup.

"*Vhat* does it look like?" barked Grandma as I coughed.

"Give that to me," hissed Enid, stomping my way. "You're going to totally ruin your lipstick."

"Here you go, you *klafte.*" Before I could blink, Grandma snatched my spoon and scooped up a matzo ball from the half-full bowl. My face lit up as she flung the giant ball at Enid. Whoot! It smacked the bitch in the face. Enid shrieked.

"How dare you!" she cried, wiping the crumbly fragments off her cheeks. Her eyes were flaring. I couldn't help laughing.

"What are you laughing at?" Enid seethed, gritting her teeth.

Rather than responding, I gave Grandma a hug. I loved this woman. She had *chutzpah!* Balls. Big ones.

Monique sprinted over to Enid. "Darling, are you okay?" she asked, flicking off bits of the dumpling from her lover's chin as if they were deadly insects. The fashion designer shot Grandma a scathing look. "What the hell did you do?"

Grinning wickedly, Grandma scooped up another perfectly formed matzo ball. *"Vould* you like to try *vun* too?"

With a gasp, Monique defensively shielded her face with her hand and turned to Enid. "Come on, darling. Let's get out of here before this dangerous woman does something to me." Wrapping her other arm around Enid, she ushered her out of the room.

"Vhat is it *vith* those two?" Grandma asked after Enid and Monique were gone.

"There's more than meets the eye."

"Oy! They *shtup vun* another?"

"So I hear."

"Vait till I tell Helen!"

Tell Grandma; tell the world. I had a hunch everyone in town would soon know about Enid's dirty little secret. And it could be the talk of the wedding. With mild amusement, I took another sip of soup.

Grandma stood up. "Bubala, feel better. Time for me to get ready for the *vedding*. I've got a hot date." She winked.

Luigi, Blake's seventy-eight-year-old tailor, had recently become Grandma's new friend with benefits. They were adorable together, and Grandma couldn't stop talking about his Italian "salami."

I thanked Grandma for coming to my rescue and gave her another big hug before she marched out of the room. I finished the rest of the soup while Monique's assistants continued working on my gown. Grandma's comic relief and the effects of her magical soup were short-lived. A stately grandfather's clock chimed five times. It was five o'clock. My parents would be landing any minute. I silently prayed they'd be here soon. Unsettling nerves again mixed with painful spasms. I could barely stand up when one of Monique's assistant asked me to take off my robe so she could help me into the altered gown. With effort, I managed. And with even greater effort, I stumbled back over to the tri-fold mirror. Yes, the taken-in dress definitely fit me more snugly, but the area where the skirt fanned out in a cascade of ruffles—it was like having a rope tied around my knees. Oh my God. I could barely take a step in the mermaid gown, which would make dancing at my wedding near impossible, let alone walking down the aisle. As I stared at my frightening bridal self, I felt like crying.

"Is there anything you can do to make it looser around here?" I asked the seamstress, tugging at the impossibly tight area.

She shook her head. "There's not enough fabric or time."

I grimaced. Not because of my disappointment but because of the relentless abdominal pain. It was getting worse. Like a hundred knives jabbing me.

In the mirror, I saw Monique's other assistant coming toward me. She was holding a jeweled creation in her hand.

"This is your bouquet. Ms. Hervé wants you to get used to holding it."

I eyed the so-called bouquet. It was a sparkling concoction of crystal starfish, pearls, and seashells. Not a fresh, fragrant bloom among them. The assistant handed me the arrangement. Grabbing it with one hand, I wasn't prepared for the weight of it. Seriously, the clunker must have weighed ten pounds. Libby had better catch it because if I missed and hit her in the head, it was going to knock her out. I fucking hated it.

My cell phone rang again. "Could you please hand me my phone," I asked the seamstress. Given how long it would take me to walk back to the couch in the constricting gown, I might miss the call. Fingers crossed, it was Blake letting me know my parents were en route. He'd arranged for a limousine to pick them up at nearby Van Nuys Airport.

"Are they on their way?" I asked Blake while Monique's two assistants took a break.

"Baby, there's a problem."

A problem? My heart hammered madly. "What's going on?"

"There's a Sig-alert."

"What do you mean?"

"A big rig toppled over. The traffic on the 101 is at a total standstill."

Oh my God! How could this be happening? "Blake, when are they going to clear it?"

I could hear Blake inhale and exhale on the other end. "I don't know. To make matters worse, it was a tanker, so there's an oil spillage too."

No, no, no, no. "Blake, is there anything you can do?" My raspy voice was thick with desperation and despair.

Silence.

"Blake, are you there?" My desperation was close to panic.

"Sorry, tiger. I got distracted. How do you feel?"

It was time to tell him the truth. Two words: "Like crap." My voice was watery. I was on the edge.

Blake: "Shit. Gotta go. Guests are showing up by the droves, and I've got to mingle with them. Hang in there, baby. I'll call you if I hear anything. Or come up with something."

"Love you," I mumbled, holding the phone limply in my hand as we ended the call. I immediately speed-dialed my father, eager to talk to him, but my phone went dead. Shit! I'd not kept it charged. And worse, I didn't have my charger with me. In my feverish stupor, I'd left it at Blake's condo. *Shit. Shit. Shit.* I now couldn't receive any updates—from either Blake or my parents.

At an all time low, I did the only thing any bride in this situation would do. Before the tri-fold mirror, I sunk to my knees, not caring if I split open my hideous gown. I couldn't help myself. I started to cry. Scratch that. I started to bawl. Big snotty, tears fell onto the jeweled bouquet as my shoulders heaved. This was my wedding day. I was sick as a dog. My dress was a mess. My parents were inaccessible. For God's sake. Couldn't one little thing go right?

I didn't know how long I'd been sobbing when I felt two warm hands on my shoulders, massaging them gently. Slowly, I lifted my head and gazed into the mirror. Squatting behind me was Blake's mother Helen, dressed to kill in her magnificent one-shoulder coral gown and a dazzling array of diamonds.

"Sweetheart, it's going to be okay. We're not starting the wedding until your parents arrive."

I met her compassionate eyes in the mirror. I looked

scarier than ever. My pale skin, now blotchy, was stained with a sea of tears, and squid-like streaks of inky mascara trickled down my cheeks.

I twitched the smallest of smiles. No words. I had no words. And then in the mirror, another figure appeared. Enid.

"It's after six o'clock. Guests are grumbling. Getting drunk on oyster shooters, which, by the way, we're running out of."

Helen cranked her long neck to face her. "Then let them drink water." The sharp tone of her voice was new to me.

Enid's face hardened. Her voice was ice-cold. "Helen, darling, I cannot disappoint our guests. I've never delayed an event. The show must go on."

Helen stood up and squarely faced Enid. "Blake and my husband are perfectly capable of entertaining *our* guests."

That was true. Both were natural-born showmen. Like father like son.

Enid's eyes narrowed. "Helen, I run the show, and I say the show must go on." She snapped her fingers. "It's as simple as that."

Helen's eyes shot back daggers. "Darling, I'm flitting the bill, and I say there's no 'show' until the McCoys get here. My future daughter-in-law is *not* walking down the aisle without her parents." She snapped her fingers. "It's as simple as *that.*"

Wow! I'd never seen Helen like this. She was in total battle-mode. A ninja warrior.

Smoke was shooting out of Enid's nostrils. I could practically smell it. "Helen, you don't seem to understand. I have a reputation to uphold. My events always go off perfectly. Without delays."

Not wasting a second, she put the walkie talkie she was holding to her mouth. "Attention. Please have the guests take their seats. The wedding is about to begin."

Helen, to my astonishment, snatched the device and put it to her mouth.

"Attention. This is Helen Bernstein. Please have the guests take their seats and make an announcement that the wedding is a little delayed." And then with force, she hurled the walkie talkie against one of the painting-lined walls. *Slam!* The little black box fell apart as it hit the floor.

"How dare you?" shrieked Enid.

Helen smiled smugly. "I've always had a good throw. You should know, I'm the designated pitcher at my annual 'Big Sister' charity softball game."

Enid was seething. "This would have never happened if Blake had married Katrina."

"Blake never wanted to marry your skanky daughter. What she did to him was abominable."

"What your son did to *her* was unforgivable. And to our family. We almost went under. Why do you think I became an event planner? Because I wanted a career?

Hardly. I needed the fucking money. We were broke. Clayton almost had to sell the house. And we had to fine-dine at Sizzler. Do you honestly think I like working for you? Hardly. You're a fucking rich bitch. Your money keeps me afloat."

"Well, Enid. You'd better think of a new *fucking* career. Because…You're…fired!" My future mother-in-law aimed her thumb and index finger at her like a gun.

Enid gasped, her mouth dropping wide open with shock. And then the unbelievable happened. On the next breath, she lunged at Helen, almost knocking her to the floor. "I hate you, you fucking bitch!" she shrieked.

Catching her balance, Helen yanked at Enid's hair. "It takes one to know one." She yanked again. Enid yelped, "Fuck you!" and retaliated. A giant clump of Enid's ebony hair—holy shit, a ten-inch hair extension!—fell to the floor, followed by a wad of Helen's platinum locks.

Before I could blink, the two women were at each other like two Siamese fighting fish. Hissing. Shrieking. Clawing. Gnawing. My eyes stayed wide as Enid ferociously tore apart the shoulder fabric of Helen's stunning dress. This hiss of the splitting silk sent goose bumps to my skin. Helen retaliated with a kick to her adversary's shin.

"I'm going to deduct the cost of this dress from

your bill," hissed Helen, now tearing at Enid's blouse while she bent down to nurse her leg. The pearl buttons popped off and—ping, ping, ping—landed close to my feet. The dueling divas continued with Enid getting the better of poor Helen after punching her hard in the gut. I'd had enough. Adrenaline pumping through my blood despite my horrible pain, I aimed my weighty jeweled bouquet at Enid and flung it like a grenade. It flew through the air and BINGO! It got her smack in the head. With a moan, she spiraled downward onto the floor. With a triumphant smile, Helen gave me a thumbs up. Her expression then contorted into one of utter disgust as she glowered at defeated Enid.

"Get up and get out of here." My soon-to-be mother-in-law's gruff voice was fueled by rage. "And don't you ever step foot on my property again. Security will escort you to the front gate."

Dazed, Enid staggered to her feet. Another voice at the doorway caught my attention. Monique. "Oh my God. My dress!" Her startled eyes darted from Helen to Enid. Panic-driven, she flitted to her disheveled, unsteady partner. "Enid, darling, what's going on here? Are you okay?"

Rubbing the back of her head, recovering Enid pinched her Botoxed face so hard a crease curled between her brows. But before she could say a word, Helen lashed out at her again.

"And you can take your *girlfriend* with you." *Holy*

cow! Helen already knew.

Enid turned crimson. Pursing her lips, she breathed loudly in and out from her nose. Her fists clenched so tightly her knuckles turned white. Finally, her mouth parted.

"Monique, darling, we're no longer needed here. Let's go." She hooked her arm into the crook of her lover's elbow. Questions begging answers danced in Monique's eyes, but she held them back. The two women stalked to the door. At the doorway, Enid turned her head and smiled wickedly. She gave Helen the evil eye.

"You and that wannabe daughter-in-law of yours will be sorry." Her icy gaze shifted to me. "Blake will never be yours, you peasant."

Her hurtful words sent a shiver up my spine. At the same time, a sharp pang stabbed my gut. I clenched my stomach and suppressed a wince as Enid and Monique slipped away. Helen took me in her arms. "Don't let her get to you, my dear. You are perfect for Blake. I'm so thrilled you're going to be my daughter-in-law. And you must absolutely promise to be on my softball team. I need a backup pitcher."

"Sure, Helen," I murmured, grateful that this incredible woman had come to my rescue. Her warm embrace was interrupted by a familiar welcomed voice.

"Honey!"

Mom! I spun around. There they were. My beloved

parents. My mother, dressed in a lovely oyster white suit, and my dad in a dapper English-style morning suit. A massive brace encased his right leg, and he was holding a spiffy cane that complemented his suit beautifully. My heart swelled with happiness. Tears of joy flooded my eyes. My mother broke away from my dad and sprinted to me. He limped behind her.

"Oh, Mom, I'm so glad you're here," I said tearfully as she gave me a maternal hug—something I'd been craving for so long. My dad was next. It felt so good to be in his arms. He smiled broadly. "I told you I was going to walk my little girl down the aisle." And here he was. He looked so handsome to me, leg brace and all.

"You look beautiful, Jennie," he said with a proud smile.

No, I don't. But his heartfelt words made me *feel* beautiful. And that was all that mattered.

My mother, with her discerning eyes, studied me. "Honey, are you all right? You look faint." My perceptive mother knew me well.

"I have a little bit of a bug." My alarmist mother immediately put her hand to my forehead. "I'm taking Advil. I'll be okay." Truthfully, now that my parents were here, everything was okay. Nothing could keep me from my wedding day.

"Where's Father Murphy?"

"He's in the backyard conferring with the Bernsteins' rabbi."

I quirked a smile. All was good.

Relaxing, my mother beamed. "Everything looks so beautiful. And guess what! I saw George Clooney and Hillary Clinton!"

My star-struck mom. I loved her so much. As for me, the only stars that mattered at my star-studded wedding were Blake…and my parents. They were here. Here at last!

Helen interjected. "I'm going to leave the three of you alone while I freshen up and change into another gown." She hugged my parents. "I'm so thrilled you made it. I'll meet you shortly along with the others in the wedding party on the veranda. The wedding of the century is about to begin."

Chapter 17

Blake

Thank fucking God, Jennifer's parents arrived safely and just in time. Standing under the shell-encrusted *chuppah* beside my best man, Jaime, and surrounded by members of the wedding party, I faced our thousand-plus guests. So many famous faces. And so many I didn't recognize. My parents' social connections could not be rivaled. Photographers were scattered everywhere, taking photos with their flash cameras. Overhead, helicopters circled the dark gray sky. News crews were trying to get the scoop on the Hollywood wedding of the century. For sure, it would be a featured story on tonight's newscasts, but I sure as hell wasn't going to tune in. Dressed in my tux, I waited anxiously for my bride. I hadn't seen her since early afternoon.

"The Wedding March" began to play. Enid had managed to install an elaborate organ—the kind you saw at Radio City Music Hall—in our backyard along with a state-of-the-art sound system. The music reverberated in my ears. To be honest, that's not the music my tiger had wanted to walk down the aisle. She had hoped to walk down to *our* song: "The First Time Ever I Saw Your Face." But Enid insisted that be our first dance song. The bitch, we'd decided, was just not worth fighting. So we compromised.

My eyes stayed glued on the veranda. Where was she? My heart hammered. Finally, a vision in white appeared on the arm of her dapper father. My tiger. My bride. My wife-to-be. She met my gaze, and a small smile curled on her lips.

The walk to the *chuppah* was a long one. And Jen walked very slowly down the winding path with her still disabled father. One baby step at a time. While Harold was beaming, her smile looked forced, her face pinched. My poor baby! I knew she felt like shit and hoped she'd taken another Advil. And I knew she wasn't thrilled about her wedding gown, but to me it was beautiful. And she was beautiful. Every eye was on her as she made her way down the aisle. Cameras and cell phones flashed.

The minutes felt like hours. As she took hesitant steps, she occasionally turned her head to acknowledge our guests. My eyes never strayed from her, and when she met my gaze, they silently told her everything was going to be all right. And that I loved her. Mind, body, and soul.

Overwhelmed with tingly emotion I'd never felt before, I just wanted her beside me. And actually thought about sweeping her off her feet and carrying her to the altar. I wanted to say our vows like it was yesterday and exchange those two magical words, "I do." We just had to get through tonight. Tomorrow, we would be on our way to the secret honeymoon destination I'd painstakingly arranged. I couldn't wait to be lying on a beach and making glorious love to my new wife on the day I turned thirty.

Chapter 18

Jennifer

Walking down the aisle, I clung to my father's arm as if it were my lifeline. Because at this very moment, it was.

Intense pain chipped away at me. Like an ax to my abdomen. I seriously felt like I was going to die.

Only one other person kept me going—Blake. *That* man who would soon be my husband. My beautiful hero, looking so handsome in his tux under a canopy of seashells and flowers. His smile and his eyes pointed at me.

Dad and I walked slowly down the aisle, each step a small victory. With my constricting gown and his leg brace, we were a perfect match. In my other hand, I held my heavy bouquet, now missing some seashells and beads. And in his, his cane.

As I took tiny steps down the aisle, I tried to acknowledge our guests. I looked left and right and then back at Blake, whose loving gaze gave me the courage to continue.

I was an emotional and physical mess. A mixture of

nerves, chills, and pain. My strapless mermaid gown was not suited for the chilly December air. Goose bumps popped along my bare arms and my teeth chattered.

Just walk and breathe. And try to smile, I told myself. *You can do it.* I forced a small smile and took in the sea of people in front of whom we were going to say our vows. But truthfully, I was treading water. Barely staying afloat. I was truly not sure I was going to make it to the altar. My father, God bless him, held me steady. I met Blake's loving gaze once more, and a sudden rush of wet heat puddled between my legs. A rush like I've never felt before.

The walk down the aisle felt like an eternity. But I made it. Dad proudly took his place beside my radiant mom, and Blake took me in his arms. I heard him whisper, "I love you."

"I love you too," I whispered back. We turned to face Rabbi Silverstein and Father Murphy.

The ceremony began. Blake clasped my free hand. His so warm, mine so icy cold. It was difficult to hear what our officiants were saying. Helicopters were hovering overhead, and the chattering of my teeth filled my ears. And then halfway through it, Blake did something so unexpected. He took off his tux jacket and gently placed it over my shoulders. I heard our guests go "ooh." Oh my Blake! My gallant Blake! But neither his hand nor his jacket could warm me up. Or make the excruciating pain go away.

The alternating words of Rabbi Silverstein and Father Murphy drifted into one ear and out the other. Whatever viral infection I'd contracted was consuming me. Another sharp spasm ripped through my body. Of all days to fall ill! I squeezed Blake's hand and bit down on my bottom lip to suppress a wince. And then another spasm and another. They grew relentless. Managing to hold on to the bouquet, I clutched my belly. A concerned Blake looked my way while our officiates continued the service.

I should have been savoring every word, but they couldn't come fast enough. We finally said our vows. With the loud chop-chop-chop of the helicopters above and my voice a mere whisper, I could barely hear myself. And Blake's sacred words were likewise washed out.

Lastly…finally…the exchange of our "I do's" and wedding bands. The latter were tied to aqua velvet pillows Marcy's eager twins were holding.

"Do you, Blake Adam Burns, take Jennifer Leigh McCoy to be your lawful wedded wife?" were the words I was longing to hear. But to my surprise, old-fashioned Father Murphy turned to the attendants and thundered, "If anyone here has any objections to this couple getting married, let them speak now or forever hold your peace."

"Yes! I do," a familiar sharp voice shouted out.

Shocked, I pivoted around. Oh my God! It was Kat! Standing up in the back of the crowd in a high-necked white goddess gown. What was she doing here? Her venomous eyes met mine and then another sharp, unbearable pain stabbed me. I clasped my lower abdomen and warm wetness met my hand. I glanced down and gasped. A rapidly expanding crimson pool was seeping through my gown.

I can't really tell you what happened next. Just this.

I heard my mother's panicked voice. "Oh, dear Lord!"

Then Grandma's. *"Oy vey iz mir!"*

And then, as I felt my knees buckle, I heard Blake shout out, "Someone call 911!"

He caught me in his arms and then everything went black.

Chapter 19

Blake

My father always said: "The only thing you can ever expect in life is the unexpected." I just didn't expect this.

I was sitting in the back of a racing ambulance, the siren blaring in my ears. Thank God, my sister Marcy was with me or I think I would have totally lost it. My heart was in my throat and my breathing was shallow. My sister squeezed my hand while my eyes stayed locked on my beautiful unconscious bride. The paramedics had told us she'd lost a lot of blood and was likely still bleeding internally. Hooked up to a portable IV and an oxygen tank, she was wrapped in a heavy blanket, which at least spared me the agony of seeing her blood-soaked wedding gown.

Foreboding thoughts bombarded me. At the top: Was I going to lose my tiger? If Kat had anything to with this, I was going to have her committed. The image of her smirking at me as I ran past her with my fallen bride in my arms flickered in my head. What the hell was she doing there? I could only surmise she flew back from Rio, and her equally mental, devious mother put her on the guest list. Without a doubt, she was still determined to stop me from marrying Jen. The sick bitch was out for blood, and I wouldn't put it past her to go as far as murder. I shuddered.

"Are you okay, Blake?" My sister's soft words cut into my dark thoughts.

I shook my head. "Marcy, I'm scared shitless." I searched her eyes for a sign that everything would be all right.

"Blake, I'm going to stay with her. We're going to do a CAT scan and go from there. Stay calm."

A KAT scan was more like it. To make sure the psycho hadn't laced my baby's veins with poison. Or stabbed her.

Fifteen agonizing minutes later, we pulled up to a private entrance to Cedars-Sinai Medical Center. We were given special treatment partly because my sister was a respected doctor there, heading up the OB/GYN department, but mostly because my family had donated enough money to have a wing named for them. My breath hitched painfully in my throat as I watched the paramedics transfer my beauty to a gurney in record speed. To my absolute horror, she began to convulse. Her tiny body was bucking up and down.

"What's happening?" I asked, my voice pure panic.

"Shit. She's going into hypovolemic shock," cried out my sister. "Someone lift up her legs. Move it! Move it!"

Nausea rose to my chest. I was so close to vomiting I was afraid to open my mouth to ask what this meant. Whatever the hell it meant, it wasn't good.

Pushing the gurney, the team of paramedics and nurses raced through the automatic doors of the hospital, with Marcy and me holding on to the railings and keeping up pace. Everything was happening so fast it was a blur.

We headed down a long corridor toward a set of double doors. The sign above them read: "MEDICAL PERSONNEL ONLY"

"Blake, you're going to have to stay here," breathed my sister as the hospital team wheeled her through. "There's a waiting room down the hall."

"No fucking way," I blurted.

"Blake, please. It's hospital regulations." Marcy looked at me imploringly.

I felt like bashing a wall, but I fought my urge and gave in.

Marcy squeezed one of my balled-up hands. "Blake, I'll let you know what's going on as soon as I can."

Five minutes later, I was slumped in an armchair in the nearby waiting room. I sunk my head between my hands and rubbed my throbbing temples. My heart was in my stomach, my breathing labored. Shit. What was taking so long? What was wrong with my tiger? Was she going to be okay? The sound of rapid footsteps cut into my mental ramblings. I looked up. Jen's parents and mine. Like me, they were all still dressed in their wedding finery. Jen's mother's eyes were all red and puffy from crying, and her father looked like he'd aged a hundred years. Worry was etched deep in my parents' faces.

"Any word?" asked my father, the most composed among us.

I could hear my jackrabbit pulse hammer in my ears. My lips pinched, I silently shook my head.

"My little girl's going to be okay," murmured Jen's father, but his words were not convincing. Tapping his cane, his arms tightened around Mrs. McCoy's trembling shoulders. She held a hand to her mouth to muffle her sobs.

I loosened my bow tie, and then squeezed my eyes shut, hoping I could make this nightmare disappear. My sister's voice brought my moment of reprieve to an abrupt end. She was now out of her bridesmaid gown and clad in green scrubs.

"We're taking Jen to surgery," she said solemnly.

I leapt to my feet. "Surgery?"

"Marcy, can you please be more specific?" asked Jen's dad, his voice shaky.

"We found a mass behind her uterus."

Still cupping her mouth, Mrs. McCoy could no longer contain herself. "Oh, dear Lord!" she sobbed. Her husband was quick to put a comforting arm around her while my mother, standing next to her, clasped her other hand.

That ruled out Kat, but confusion mixed with fear. My voice faltered. "But she told me everything was okay after her visit with you."

Marcy pressed her lips thin. "Blake, she was. The ultrasound didn't detect this."

"Fuck." *Fuck, fuck, fuck.*

Marcy continued. "I'm heading up to surgery now."

"Can we see her before she goes?" spluttered Jen's mom through her tears.

"I'm afraid not. She's already in transit. The operation will likely last three hours. I suggest you all get some rest."

Three hours? I wasn't sure if I was going to last that long.

Her eyes soaked, Jennifer's mom asked if there was a chapel in the hospital. She and her husband wanted to go there to pray.

Pray. That's all we could do. I was going there too.

Chapter 20

Blake

"N o, no, stop! Please don't hurt me!"

My eyes snapped open. Jen was screaming in her sleep. All hooked up to tubes and monitors, she writhed in her hospital bed, her voice a hoarse whimper.

Alarmed, I bolted from the bedside chair where I'd fallen asleep. I was still in my tux shirt, though I'd unbuttoned it and chucked the bow tie. In a frightened heartbeat, I was by her side. She must be having one of her Springer nightmares. I smoothed her damp hair, my fingertips grazing her forehead. Her skin burnt beneath my touch. She was hot. I hoped she didn't have a fever. A sign of infection. Sweat beads laced her pale skin. She looked as if all her blood had been drained from her. My poor tiger. She'd been through so much.

Sunlight streamed into the room. It was morning, so I thought. I was dazed myself. Last night's events whirled around in my head, but clarity quickly filled my mind. My baby had had surgery. The lengthy operation had gone well, my sister said. With no complications.

Both my parents and Jen's had anxiously hung out at the hospital until they could see her in recovery. It was going on midnight. Once they saw her resting peaceful-ly, despite all the tubes and monitors she was hooked up to, my sister insisted everyone go home. There was nothing we could do at this point. Jen's tearful mom didn't want to leave, but Harold convinced her it was in everyone's best interest. My parents drove the McCoys to our house where they were staying. Only I stayed behind. I needed to be here for my Jen when she came to. She was transferred to her own private room—a slick suite that looked more like it belonged in a five-star hotel than a hospital. My baby deserved the best. The hospital staff was kind enough to provide me a cot, but I couldn't take my eyes off her. Despite being hooked up to all sorts of gizmos, she looked so peaceful. Like an angel with her long satin curls fanned out across the fluffy pillow. I was mesmerized by her beauty, the rise and fall of her chest, and every soft breath. Leaning over her, I gently traced a finger over her warm silky lips—those lips that had set my heart and soul on fire. I relived that first kiss—a kiss from a spunky, blindfolded girl that had forever changed my life. A kiss that had made me love and need someone more than the air I breathed. Memories of all our good times together danced in my head. Our wedding was not among them.

As I watched her breathe into the wee hours of the

morning, the fragility of life hit me like a plane going down. How fast and suddenly it could be taken away. Though she'd pulled through the operation, there was one big unanswered question. I tried to force it to the back of mind, but it weighed on my heart until sleep finally took hold of me.

Her hallucinatory screams catapulted me back to the moment. I was expecting to awaken to my sleeping beauty. Not this. She continued to twist and turn. I caressed her tortured face as she feverishly shook it side to side.

"Jen, Jen, it's me. It's okay. I'm here. Do you hear me?" I tried to sound calm but inside panic gripped me. With my free hand, I pushed the call button for a nurse or doctor.

I continued to say her name, my voice desperate, and stroke her hair. Finally, her eyes fluttered opened and met mine. Oh, those beautiful green orbs! I was so happy to see them. She calmed, but a mixture of terror and confusion was still etched deep on her face.

"Blake," she whispered, her voice a mere rasp. "Where am I? What happened?"

It was so good to hear her voice as faint as it was. It took all I had not to shed a tear. I tenderly kissed her warm forehead, my lips on fire from the mere touch of her flesh. I gazed at her lovingly and reverently. Her bewildered eyes stayed fixed on mine.

"Tiger, you're at Cedars. You were hemorrhaging.

You had to have an operation."

"Surgery?" Fear flickered in her eyes.

I nodded.

"What did they do?" Her voice was so small.

My heart was splintering. Should I tell her? My father always said the truth is the best medicine. I swallowed hard.

"Jen, baby, you had a partial hysterectomy."

Her eyes blinked several times. "Meaning what?"

I chewed my lip. I fucking didn't want to tell her. "Meaning they found a mass on your uterus and had to remove part of it along with one of your ovaries."

Silence. I was expecting tears, but none materialized.

"Does that mean I can't have babies?"

My lips pressed together in a thin dismal line. "I don't know." While I knew how much my tiger wanted to give me a den full of little cubs, I'd always love her whether we had children or not. And that wasn't what was eating at my heart. She read my anxious face.

"Do I have cancer?" Her tiny voice was stoic. Oh, my brave tiger.

My heart was shredding. I was so close to shedding tears. "I don't know. They're doing a biopsy. The results should be back in the afternoon."

"Okay," she murmured.

No, it was so not fucking okay. What had I done wrong to deserve this fate? It shouldn't have been her.

My angel. No way.

Sparing me from saying another word, a nurse walked into the room. Petite, she looked Filipino and was wearing a cheery pink smock.

"Ah!" she said brightly. "You're awake, Ms. McCoy."

Ms. McCoy. My heart stuttered. Damn it. She was supposed to be Mrs. Burns this morning. And I was supposed to be fucking her brains out on our honeymoon, though right now that didn't matter. My tiger was alive. And that's all that counted.

Without wasting a second, the nurse, whose name was Wanda, plunged one of those high-tech thermometers into her ear, took her pulse, and checked her charts. I held my breath.

"She has a slight fever; nothing to be alarmed about. All her other vitals seem normal."

I blew out a sharp breath of relief. Now, if only her biopsy came back normal. I silently prayed to God.

"I'd like to sponge her down," said the sweet nurse, cranking up her bed so my tiger was in a semi-sitting position. Her locks of hair curled like ribbons along the pillow.

"May I do that?" I implored while she ambled to the bathroom.

"I don't see why not," she replied, a slight chuckle in her accented voice.

She returned from the lavatory with a wet washcloth

in her hand. She handed it to me. "Here you go," she said with a smile. "Just be careful around her incision. I'll be back soon with something for Ms. McCoy to eat."

I thanked the sweet nurse and began to wash my tiger, beginning with her face. Gently, I traced the warm wet cloth around it. She closed her eyes.

"Are you okay, baby?"

She replied with a weak nod.

"Do you hurt?"

"Just a little. But I feel so weak and nauseous."

The pain meds were doing their job, but I was concerned about her queasiness.

"You lost a lot of blood. Marcy had to give you a transfusion."

As I made my way down her slender arms, she blinked open her eyes. "Marcy?"

"Yeah. My sister was the surgeon. She's the best there is. She saved your life."

A small smile curled on her lips. The first since she'd regained consciousness. "Blake, I need to thank her."

I smiled back at her. "I'm sure she'll be here shortly."

I lowered her thin blanket down to her ankles. She looked so thin. So frail. Gingerly, I lifted her hospital gown, and for the first time, I saw where the incision was. A large thick bandage covered the area—just below her abdomen. My tiger's beautiful breasts quivered. She managed to take a peek.

"Guess I won't be wearing a bikini again."

I laughed. Only my tiger could make me do that when I wanted to fucking cry.

"I hear one-pieces are 'in' this year. And truthfully, tiger, I'd rather see you wearing nothing."

She squeezed my free hand. "Oh, Blake. I love you so much." And then the floodgates broke loose. Tears streamed down her cheeks.

"Baby, what's the matter?" Panic gripped me by my balls.

"Oh, Blake, what if I have cancer? I don't want to leave you."

I dabbed her tears away with the cloth. "Stop it, baby. You're a tiger. You're going to get through this." I paused. "*We're* going to get through this, do you understand?"

Thank fucking God, I had some acting skills. On the outside, I stayed calm, but inside I was cracking. I felt so fucking powerless. I was *that* man who was supposed to protect her and save her from the evils of the world, but this time her superhero couldn't save her from the uncontrollable and unknown.

She nodded, the tears still falling. And then she smiled again, this time a real smile, and held my gaze in hers. With her hand, she traced the outline of my jaw.

"Happy Birthday, Blake."

Balls. I'd totally forgotten it was my thirtieth birthday. And then I remembered what I'd wanted. It was plain and simple. I'd wanted to wake up to my wife. Start the next decade of my life with the girl I loved with my heart, my body, and my soul.

Damn it, I was going to make that happen. So, my bride was wearing a hospital gown instead of a wedding gown, but right now that was the most beautiful dress in the world. I lowered my lips to hers and let her know how much I loved her. Weak as she was, she didn't resist. She cradled my head between her hands, her hot tears warming my face. Warming every part of me. Today, Jennifer McCoy was going to become Jennifer Burns.

Chapter 21

Jennifer

Calamity Jen.

That's what Libby often called me. Aptly.

My wedding had been the biggest calamity of my life. A disaster. I'd totally fucked it up. Let down my future husband. His parents. My parents. And over a thousand guests.

"I'm sorry I screwed everything up," I sniffled as I forced myself to break away from Blake's passionate kiss.

Blake gently brushed away my tears. "Stop it, tiger. It's not your fault."

"But all those people…all that money your parents spent…"

"Fuck the money, baby. My parents won't miss it. And except for our families and close friends, those people mean nothing to me. Or to us."

The bubbly nurse, who'd returned, made me drink some water. Blake held the cup as I sipped it through a straw. The cool liquid felt good against my parched palate and raw throat. Then another cheerful hospital attendant pranced into the room with a breakfast tray. A light meal of scrambled eggs, toast, and juice.

"Eat," Blake ordered, sitting on the edge of my bed.

With my fatigue, nausea, and the results of the biopsy weighing on my heart, I had no appetite, but I took a few bites to make Blake happy. I'd much rather be holding his hand than a fork.

My eyes grew heavy. Blake ruffled my hair and gave me a light kiss on my forehead. "Baby, rest. I'm not going anywhere." A faint smile spread on my lips as I closed my eyes.

I don't know how long I'd been out when my eyes blinked open. Blake was still there seated beside me. But standing beside him was a tall, lanky long-haired young man with warm twinkly eyes who bore a striking resemblance to Jesus. He was clad in a long white robe with a notched high collar and holding a pamphlet in one hand. A priest? Nurse Wanda was in the room too. My blood ran cold and my heart beat as fast as a hummingbird's wings. Something was wrong. Terribly wrong. *Cancer.* Was he here to read me my last rites?

"Blake, are we saying goodbye?" I stammered.

That dazzling mischievous smile I loved so much lit up his face. "No, baby, we're saying our vows."

My heart continued to beat in a frenzy while he introduced us. Reverend Dooby was a newly ordained Universal Life Church minister. We were all God's children. A shocking but beautiful reality swept over me like a warm summer shower. We were getting married.

In my drugged-out haze, the reverend's laid-back voice drifted in my ears like a magic carpet. It was some New Age ceremony with words like love, peace, and harmony abounding. Blake held my hand, his eyes never leaving me.

The reverend came to the end of his pamphlet. "Do you, Blake Burns, take this beautiful babe to be your wife?"

"I do." Blake smiled.

"And do you, Jennifer McCoy, take this handsome dude to be your husband?"

"I do," I whispered, my eyes watering. So much for Shakespeare.

Reverend Dooby closed his pamphlet. "Yo, bro, it's ring time."

My eyes stayed glued on Blake as he dipped a hand into a side pocket of his tuxedo pants. To my utter surprise, two SpongeBob Band-Aids appeared. He looked at me sheepishly.

"Sorry, baby. Borrowed these from the children's ward. Marcy's twins still have our rings so they'll have to do for now."

Oh my Blake! My smiling lips quivered as he hand-ed me one. Then, he gently lifted my left hand, which fortunately wasn't hooked up to IVs. A tear rolled down my cheek as he wrapped the Band-Aid around my ring finger just above my magnificent engagement ring. The brilliant snowflake diamond sparkled in the ray of sunshine that beamed through the curtains.

It was my turn. My hands trembling, I copied his actions and wrapped the other Band-Aid around his left fourth finger. With a cheek to cheek grin, he admired my handiwork.

Reverend Dooby's voice echoed in my ears. "I now pronounce you husband and wife."

We were married! Blake gently drew me close to him. His mouth pressed on mine in a passionate embrace I wanted never to end. Our tongues danced and our bodies melted into one. We had just vowed to spend the rest of our lives together...to cherish each other until death do us part. I felt no pain as my fear succumbed to everlasting love.

The sobs of Nurse Wanda brought me back to the moment. "I'm sorry. I always cry at weddings. But this one is so special." Her tears were contagious. I was crying too.

Breaking the eternal kiss, I held my new husband's breathtaking face in my hands.

His eyes bore into mine "Mrs. Burns, thank you for the best birthday present ever."

"Oh, Blake, how can I ever top it?"

"By asking me the same question next year."

Chapter 22

Blake

The McCoys showed up a couple of hours after our nuptials. Nurse Wanda was back in the room, taking Jen's temperature.

"Good news, Mrs. Burns, your temperature is back to normal."

Mrs. Burns. Man, I loved those two words. And hoped I'd be hearing them for the rest of my life. Jen's prognosis was still gnawing away at me. My stomach was twisted in a knot.

Jen smiled sheepishly at her parents. "Mom, Dad…Blake and I have something to tell you." She shot me a look asking for a go-ahead. I nodded. Mrs. McCoy bit her lip, expecting bad news. My tiger continued.

"Um…uh…we got married this morning." She proudly held up her hand to show off her marriage "band"-Aid. I proudly did the same.

A warm smile spread across Harold's face while his wife exploded into tears.

Jen furrowed her brows. "Oh, Mom. Are you mad at me?"

Jen's mother reached into her small handbag for a lacy hankie. Dabbing at her tears, she rushed to Jen's bed and hugged her. "Oh, honey, your dad and I are so happy for the both of you. We love you so much."

A dazzling smile flashed on Jen's face. "I love you both so much too."

Mr. McCoy shook my hand. "Welcome to the family, son."

About an hour later, Libby and Chaz showed up while her parents were grabbing a bite to eat at the hospital cafeteria. Thrilled to hear about our marriage, they brightened Jen's spirits and kept her distracted. Especially Chaz, who made Jen laugh so hard it hurt. While waiting at the head of the long valet line for his car after the wedding fiasco, Kat had cut in front of him. He did what he'd always wanted to do. He slapped the rude psycho bitch. Way to go, my man!

Feeling a little stronger, Jen told us about the catfight between my mother and Kat's. Man, I would have given my left foot to see my mother kick Enid's ass. And score one for my tiger for almost knocking the bitch out. Despite my gloom, I laughed *my* ass off with Jen's best friends. I had newfound respect for my mother, the warrior.

Libby and Chaz spent a half hour with us. Shortly after they left, the McCoys returned to the room, and my parents and Grandma showed up. Jen and I shared the news about our marriage with my family. They were thrilled, especially Grandma who exclaimed, *"Zei gezunt.* So *vhen* are you going to make me some beautiful grandchildren?"

My heart skittered. *From her lips to God's ears.*

My mother pecked my cheek. "Congratulations, darling. And happy birthday. I brought along the perfect cake to celebrate."

Only my mother would think about my birthday at a time like this. Before I could say another word, in walked two burly hospital attendants, wheeling in our twenty-layer ocean-themed wedding cake—complete with multi-colored macaroon shellfish dotting the pearl-white frosting. For sure, thirty candles were lit among the many layers. I mentally rolled my eyes. But I had to love her.

"Following Meg's excellent suggestion, we took the rest of the reception food to a homeless shelter. But we decided to keep the cake. Whatever's not eaten, we'll give to the hospital staff."

My mother and Jen's exchanged warm smiles. My mother meant well. She cared about people. She cared about me.

"Now, darling boy, make a wish and blow out the candles."

"Candles *shmandles.* Such a *vaste* of time," growled Grandma as I prepared to do the honors.

There was only one wish to make. You know it. Drawing in a deep breath, I blew out the candles. All thirty with my pursed mouth and puffed out cheek*s*.

Together, Jen and I sliced the first piece of cake, my strong hand cupping her limp one. My birthday cake was our wedding cake and vice versa. In wedding tradition, we fed each other a mouthful and moaned.

I thought about my wish. *Oh baby, stay with me.*

The minutes crawled by. Every hour felt like an eternity. Jen dozed on and off while we anxiously awaited the biopsy report. I was on pins and needles. Every fifteen minutes, I texted my sister who texted back with the same two words: *No news.* Let me tell you, patience was not one of my virtues.

Finally at five p.m., a little after Jen awoke from a nap, Marcy ambled into the room. It now resembled a florist's shop with all the beautiful fragrant flowers sent over by friends of my parents. Clad in a white lab coat, she was holding a clipboard with some papers attached to it. I couldn't read her expression—it was a total poker face. My stomach clenched. She glanced down at the charts.

"I'm afraid…"

Oh fuck. God, no! My racing heart was about to beat out of my chest.

"…Jennifer is going to be stuck with my brother for a very long time."

It took me a second to deconstruct her words. And when I heard her utter the magic word "benign," I swear my cock did a happy dance.

In my haze of over-the-top happiness, I could hear Jen's mother weeping, "Thank you, good Lord. Thank you."

I rushed to my tiger's side. I took her into my arms. "Did you hear that, baby? You're going to be okay."

Her glistening eyes searched mine. "Blake, why are you crying?"

Balls. Blake A-for-Alpha Burns was an emotional car wreck. I'd held back tears of sorrow, but I couldn't hold back tears of joy.

She kissed away my tears. Whoever said real men don't cry needed to have their fucking head examined.

Chapter 23

Blake

My tiger was released from the hospital on Christmas Day. It was the best Christmas present I could have gotten. While she was frail, she was home and on the road to recovery. And we were husband and wife. We were now wearing our matching platinum wedding bands. Marcy had brought them to the hospital. They were both inscribed with one word: "Forever."

"Merry Christmas, Mr. and Mrs. Burns," said the cheerful doorman as I helped my slow-moving but radiant wife into our building. "Surprised to see you back from your honeymoon so soon."

"A little change in plans," I replied. Jen giggled.

When I got to my apartment, I unlocked the door and then swept my tiger into my arms.

Jen gazed up at me. "What are you doing, Blake? You know, I can walk."

I rolled my eyes at her and kicked the door open. "Jeez, tiger. Tradition. I'm carrying you across the threshold."

A big smile flashed on her wan face, and she smacked a kiss on my lips. "Oh, Blake, you're such a romantic. But please don't make me laugh because it hurts!"

Jen's eyes lit up when I carried her into the living room. I'd managed to score a Christmas tree at the last minute at a lot not far from Cedars. A last minute deal that nobody wanted, it was smallish and kind of scruffy like an undernourished rescue dog. When I spotted it, I knew it was mine. Just like my Jen, it was a survivor and needed TLC. Jen's mom, God bless her, rushed to Rite-Aid and scored some bulbs and decorations at fifty percent off. The tree, I must say, was shining brightly just like my tiger.

"Oh, Blake!" she exclaimed as I set her down on the couch. "You got me a Christmas tree?"

"No. I got *us* one. Merry Christmas, Mrs. Burns."

"The same, Mr. Burns."

I lowered myself onto the couch next to her. She snuggled against me, folding her legs over mine and resting her head on my shoulder. Her knees grazed my cock. I inhaled the intoxicating cherry-vanilla scent of her hair and then kissed her scalp lightly. It felt so good to cuddle her.

"Baby, I'm sorry I don't have a Christmas present for you." The truth: we were supposed to be on our honeymoon, and I was going to surprise her with something special. I still hadn't shared that destination with her, nor was I planning to.

Lifting her head, she cradled my face in her hands. "Wrong. I have you, baby. The best Christmas present a girl could ever hope for."

Impulsively, I pulled her face to mine. I crushed my lips against hers and wasted no time making the kiss hotter and deeper. Maybe she couldn't fuck, but she sure could kiss.

Jen's parents came over for dinner as did mine. So did Grandma and Marcy, minus her twins. My nephews stayed at home with their nanny, preferring to play with the boxload of 3D Nintendo games I'd bought them for Chanukah.

Jen's mom made her traditional Irish stew, and Grandma brought over a pot of her matzo ball soup. My tiger ate voraciously, and it pleased me. Her healthy appetite signaled she was getting better.

Respecting Jennifer's fragile state of health, our guests didn't linger. After I cleaned up with everyone's help, Jen and I curled up on the couch and watched a Netflix movie. *Frozen.* The very flick we'd seen last Christmas day when I'd showed up at her house in Boise and surprised her. She loved this movie. And just like before, she cried her eyes out. It so fucking turned me on. And it gave me an idea. I had to admit. Sometimes, I was a fucking genius. No pun intended.

We welcomed the New Year in together with what we decided would be an annual tradition—we boiled two lobsters. Jen named hers Kat, and I named mine Enid. Over champagne, we toasted to our new life together.

Jen recovered slowly but steadily. As much as she wanted to get back to work, I made her stay home an extra week just to play it safe. And when she finally did go into the office, we drove there together as Jen was not permitted to drive for the rest of the month.

The hardest part was that we couldn't fuck—specifically, I couldn't sink my cock into her pussy or her ass. We had to get the okay from Marcy that she was fully healed internally and that might take up to two months. That's not to say that my cock didn't get any action. We got creative and I fucked her every other way I knew how. And lucky for Jen, her clit was not off bounds. Nor were sex toys if they were used externally. By the time what we hoped would be Jen's final visit to my sister, she was jokingly complaining that her jaw was strained, her fingers calloused, and that her cleavage and her armpits, my substitute pockets of paradise, were chafed. She'd also had to replace the batteries of all our sex toys. And she was positive her healthy weight gain could be attributed to all the high caloric cum she'd swallowed. I actually believed her.

On Friday, February the thirteenth, the day before Valentine's Day, I insisted on accompanying Jen to her morning appointment with Marcy. Hopefully, it would be her last. Jen caved in, but made me sit in the waiting room. I was the sole male in a sea of women, several very attractive, and felt a little conspicuous when I caught their eyes on me. I gave them a little wave and told them I was here with my wife. God, I loved saying that word. They responded in unison with a disappoint-ed chorus of "Ohs" and went back to their cell phones and magazines. I took out my iPhone, but while I answered some e-mails, my mind wandered.

It was strange to think of my sister examining my wife. Exploring parts that were meant only for me. In my mind's eye, I pictured Jen in those stirrups, legs spread wide, her perfectly preened pink pussy in full view. My cock flexed. I had the burning urge to bust through the door and fuck her on the examining room table. But the thought of my sister watching quickly put that fantasy to rest though I was still horny as hell. Fingers crossed Jen would be cleared to have real sex. It had been way too long—in fact, the longest my cock had gone without pussy in my entire adult life. Twenty long minutes later, the receptionist broke into my wet dreams and told me my sister wanted to see me in her office. My heart accelerating, I leapt up from my chair.

Jennifer was already seated in Marcy's office when

I came flying in. A smile sparkled on her face. Marcy, seated behind her desk, lifted her recently acquired reading glasses onto her head.

"Hi, babe. How'd it go?" I asked, taking the chair right next to Jen's and sounding on edge.

"Great news."

Marcy took over. "Yes, Jennifer has healed beautifully. The two of you can resume sexual intercourse immediately."

Immediately? Like could I fuck Jennifer over Marcy's desk right here and now? "Seriously?" I asked incredulously.

Jen squeezed my hand. "Really, baby."

My cock jumped with joy, but at the same time, a cocktail of apprehension and anxiety seeped through my veins. While I'd counted down the days to sink my cock into my tiger, unsettling questions hammered my brain. Could I hurt her? Tear her apart? Make her bleed? "Will there be any complications?" I asked Marcy, thinking maybe we should do it in one of her examining rooms for the first time just in case. Again, that image of fucking my wife in those stirrups flashed in my mind.

Jen answered my question. "Marcy says you can do it as hard as you want."

Nodding, my sister smiled at me sheepishly. My cock was doing a happy dance.

"Yes!" I said with a victorious air punch. The two

of us were taking the day off from work. Boss's orders.

And then if I couldn't be flying higher, Marcy shared one other bit of good news.

Let me rephrase. It was the best fucking news I'd heard all year.

Holy crap! I was ready to pass out the cigars.

And then I did something I should have done a long time ago. Before Jen's smiling eyes, I hugged my sister.

I drove home like a mad man. Skimming red lights and exceeding the speed limit.

"Blake, what the hell are you doing?" shouted Jen, her ponytail whipping across her face. "You're going to get us killed."

"Getting us home."

Ten short minutes later, I zipped into my condo driveway and brought my Porsche to a screeching halt. I literally jumped over my passenger door and yanked Jennifer out. Grasping her hand, I raced past the wide-eyed doorman to the elevator. A press of a button and a ping. The elevator doors parted, and in one swift move, I hauled her into the car and shoved her against a wall. My body pressed against hers in a heated fit of desire and need.

"Blake, I can't breathe," Jen panted out as the elevator doors closed.

"In a few minutes, you won't be walking either," I panted back, gnawing her everywhere and rubbing my already stiff cock against her belly. I slid my hand into the waistband of her jeans and glided my fingers between her legs.

"Jeez, Jen. You're so fucking hot and wet," I breathed against her neck as I maneuvered my middle finger into her entrance. Fuck, she felt good. She fisted my hair and moaned.

"You okay, babe?" I asked, still anxious.

"Yes," she breathed out. "Blake, I don't think we're moving."

She was right. I slammed the palm of my free hand against my floor button and the elevator ascended. I pumped my finger up and down Jen's tunnel. It was dripping wet. Intact.

"Blake, are you going to fuck me in the elevator?"

"I may have to." Dry humping her while I finger fucked her was setting my cock on fire.

Fortunately, the elevator reached our floor with no stops.

Two desperate minutes later, we were stripped to the bone and I was on top of her. My throbbing cock was rock-hard and so fucking ready, but I wanted to taste-test her first—warm her up for me. I spread her legs and then raised myself so I was kneeling between them. Not wasting a second, I went down on her, inhaling the sweet smell of her sex. After flicking and licking her slick folds, I powered my tongue deep inside her. A loud moan escaped her throat.

"Oh God, Blake. So good," she cried out, arching up against my hungry mouth.

So good. Just the words I wanted to hear. I began to fuck her with my tongue, driving in and out of her without abandon. She bucked wildly against my face, her moans turning into melodic whimpers. The fact that she was so sexually responsive was sending me over the moon and making my swelling cock ache with desire. I moved one hand to her clit and rubbed it vigorously. Jen's whimpering morphed into screams as she headed toward orgasm. Her fingernails clawed my skin. The pain mixed with the pleasure I was giving her and was driving me crazy with lust.

A heartbeat later, she succumbed and juddered around my tongue while my taste buds melted in her delicious juices.

Letting her ride out her orgasm, I withdrew my tongue and lifted my head to get a look at her. Still breathing heavily, she looked good and fucked. Now, it was my turn. My cock was ready for its grand entrance, but I had to admit I was suffering from stage fright. The questions I'd pondered in my sister's office whirled around again in my head. I was still afraid of hurting her with my monstrous cock. And new insecurities surfaced. Could I still fill her to the hilt? Would she feel me? Would she come for me around my cock like the tiger she was?

I repositioned us so that I was hovering over her on the balls of my feet, my hands anchored by her head and holding me up. Her legs were now bent and raised like a happy baby, her ankles hooked around my neck. Somehow, that stirrup fantasy lurked in my head. My anxious cock was lined up with her pussy.

"Baby, I want you to insert my cock into your pussy." I wasn't taking any chances. Despite my sister's assurances, I feared I would rip my tiger apart with a forceful thrust and my size.

My eyes stayed on her beautiful, impassioned face as she fisted my big cock, her fingers barely able to meet. It twitched with anticipation upon feeling the crown at her entrance. The build-up of being back inside her had my blood racing.

"Baby, take your sweet time," I moaned as she slid my cock, inch by thick inch, into her warm wet chasm. Oh, God yes! She was doing it—taking me to the hilt. I let out a hiss when my cock hit her womb.

"Blake, do I feel okay?" Worry was etched on her face.

"Oh, fuck, yes, baby. Better than ever."

A smile of relief curled on her lips as she clenched her muscles around my pulsing shaft. My brave tiger hadn't told me she was as anxious as me. Up until now, neither of us knew if the surgery had any physical impact on her.

"Am I hurting you?" I asked nervously as I slowly withdrew.

"Oh Blake, you feel amazing. I've missed you so much."

"The same, baby." Relief crashed through me. It felt so fucking good to be home. I thrust my cock back into her, ready to ravish her. But I controlled my strokes, starting off slowly, and then gradually picked up my pace. A look of rapture washed over her face.

"Faster, harder, Blake! I'm not going to break."

In no time, I was pounding into her, ruthlessly and relentlessly. You'd think my cock would have no stamina after two months with no pussy, but let me tell you, Mr. Burns was blessed with muscle memory. There are fucks. And there are epic fucks. We were heading toward the latter. My cock was in overdrive, and every magic spot was within striking distance.

She clutched my biceps to give her more leverage and rocked her hips into mine with each powerful thrust. I'd almost forgotten how fucking fantastic it felt to fuck her. She was so tight, so wet, so hot. And so mine.

"Don't stop," she panted out.

"Don't worry, baby. Not a chance in hell." I wasn't going to stop hammering her until the elderly, hard-of-hearing couple next door was calling security.

Our eyes never lost contact. Her face flushed with lust as my cock continued to plunder her sweet pussy. I

grunted and growled. She howled. There was something so urgent and savage about this position that
brought out our inner animals. My insatiable tiger was
back, and my cock was back where it belonged with
feral ferocity.

I had newfound respect for the men who served our
country. Especially those stationed on ships in the
middle of nowhere or twenty thousand leagues under
the sea in submarines. I mean, how the fuck did they do
it? Months away from loved ones and no pussy. They
all deserved medals of honor for their courage and
bravery. I was about to get a medal of my own. I'd
never lasted this long. Deep inside, I never wanted her
to let me go.

And then unexpectedly, she began to sob, "Oh God,
oh God," and my fears bounced back into my head.

"Tell me you're okay, baby." Borderline panic.

She nodded feverishly. "Yes, yes, yes! Oh Blake,
I'm about to come!"

My balls retracted as she began to convulse around
my pulsating cock. On the roar of my name, I slammed
into her one more time and my own massive orgasm
assaulted me. I'm talking nuclear. My whole body
jerked as my hot release showered her magnificent
pussy. Our half-mast eyes stayed locked in a haze of
passion.

While my cum spilled into her, my heart filled with
a deep love for the woman who was my wife. For the

woman who would one day be the mother of our children. I crushed my mouth on her parted lips.

After a few luscious minutes, I withdrew from her. I rolled onto my back and shifted her so her head was resting on my chest. She was still sobbing.

"Why are you crying, baby?" I asked, brushing away her hot tears.

"Oh, Blake. That was so amazing, but I was so afraid. Afraid we wouldn't have what we had."

I caressed the top of her head. "Baby, I was a little freaked out too." Am I fucking kidding? I was scared shitless. "But what we have now is greater than what we had before. That was the best fuck I've ever had."

My words didn't stop the tears, but they did put a bright smile on her face. I drew her tight against me. We stayed in that position for several long, blissful minutes, neither of us saying another word. Jen finally broke the soulful silence. Her tears had subsided.

"Blake, we should shower and head into the office," whispered my diligent and so talented wife.

"No, Mrs. Burns, we're going to work from home today."

And trust me, we had our work cut out for us.

And a lot of catching up to do.

We fucked all day. All night. And all through the next.

The. Best. Valentine's. Day. Ever.

Chapter 24

Jennifer

I sobbed out my orgasm. Loud, heaving, sobs that to the unknowing ear might have been construed as the sounds of someone grieving a lost loved one.

They were just the opposite. The sobs of ecstasy. Of someone who was spilling with love and pleasure so intense it couldn't be measured.

Oh, my Blake. He had made glorious love to me. Fucked me with such care and reverence. Letting me put his cock inside me with my trembling fingers. Waiting until he knew I could take him to the limit before he started to thrust. And those first strokes were so tender and slow. Like he was caressing my pussy. And then he took me as if he owned me because he did. As my orgasm took over, like the waves of a tsunami taking everything in its wake, every worry I'd had washed out to sea. My eyes had stayed locked on his impassioned, glistening face as he'd watch me come and simultaneously grunted out his own climax of cataclysmic proportions.

And then we'd talked. Shared our insecurities and

fears. Blake's honesty and vulnerability struck a deep chord in my heart. Yes, we both didn't really know what to expect and we'd avoided the touchy topic, but I had an idea. Unbeknownst to him, I'd done a lot of research online about what sex was like after a hysterectomy. Some said it was better, but most women complained about pain and the loss of sensation. Since I'd had only a partial hysterectomy, I was hoping I'd be in the former group, but there was no guarantee or way of finding out beforehand. When Marcy gave me the clearance that it was okay to have sex, I should have done a happy dance. Instead, I was a nervous wreck. I just didn't let Blake know that.

Blake held me close to him, his heart beating like a love song in my ear. The silence that followed transported me to another place. I felt not only a physical and emotional connection to him, but also a spiritual one that couldn't be put into words. We'd at last consummated our marriage. He belonged to me and I belonged to him. We'd put the needs of the other before our own. He didn't just make me a better person. He made me the best I could be. Tears of pure bliss streamed down my face. We were husband and wife.

The days and months that followed flew by and were the happiest of my life. Blake and I settled into a routine of work hard, play hard, and fuck hard.

We saw his family a lot. Every Shabbat, we went to his parents' house and one Friday night, his grandma came over and helped me do it at our place. I was taking a course at the local synagogue on Jewish holidays and customs and was even contemplating studying Hebrew. Whether I'd convert or not was still up in the air, but these endeavors made me closer to Blake and his family.

We socialized a lot too, though we were trying to cut back on the number of galas and premiers Blake got invited to. Yes, we ran into his former hook-ups more times than we wished, but I was quickly gaining self-confidence as Mrs. Blake Burns. We even ran into Kitty-Kat, who gave me predatory stares but stayed faraway from us, knowing what I damn well could and would do to her. I kept her phone with the *Fuck the Bitch* footage in a safety deposit box. And had a spare copy.

We went out often with Gloria and Jaime. And sometimes along with their adorable twins who were now walking and talking. It was so cute the way they called us Jen-Jen and Bwake. Blake and I talked a lot about having kids of our own though we both knew that journey was not going to be a typical or easy one.

We also socialized quite frequently with Blake's sister Marcy and her twins. She'd saved my life and I was forever beholden to her. The little monsters were not monsters at all—just two rambunctious little boys who enjoyed watching cartoons and playing board games as much as I did; they loved SpongeBob, but still couldn't beat me at Junior Scrabble. To my utter delight, Blake had grown much closer to his sister and his nephews, and we were both there for her when she had to contend with her ex. The wedding present she had promised us was beyond our belief. No price tag could be put on it.

I was still attending my weekly support group for rape victims. Blake's wonderful mom was organizing a benefit in the Fall that would raise a ton of money and help us expand our reach out program as well as move to safer headquarters. Jeffrey, her new event planner, was overseeing it. That was one gala Blake and I wouldn't miss.

And once a week, I got together with my best friend Libby for a girls' night out. She'd flown to France and broken up with her longtime boyfriend Everett. Though saddened, she was handling it pretty well. Blake had a friend he wanted to fix her up with, but right now, she just wanted to be single and concentrate on her career.

The only people I missed seeing regularly were my parents. They'd come to visit me one more time while I was recuperating from my surgery, but once I'd fully recovered, we Skyped and then they embarked on their dream trip—sailing to Europe on the Queen Mary. They e-mailed me daily and sent me many postcards from their month-long travels abroad. Dad's leg had completely healed, and they were having the time of their lives. I couldn't be happier for them. I told Blake that if our schedules allowed, I wanted us to visit them in Boise sometime in the summer.

Work was amazing; I loved my job. My block of telenovelas based on bestselling erotic romances was a huge success; the ratings had gone through the roof—skyrocketed—and had even exceeded analysts' expectations. At the May Upfront in New York, Blake and I announced that MY-SIN TV was being spun off into a 24/7 cable channel. The audience of advertisers and affiliates exploded with excitement. In addition to airing more telenovelas, we were expanding the block with reality programming and talk shows targeted at women. Leading it off in the morning was one of the programs I'd proudly developed. Rather than telling the audience about it, Blake and I had decided to give them a sneak peek. The curtain rose behind us, and there was Grandma and her erotic book club heatedly arguing about who was the sexiest book boyfriend—among them, Christian Grey, Jesse Ward, and Lucien Knight. "*Oy!* That Lucien!" quipped Grandma. "Trust me, any Viking *shmiking* who can get his *shmekel* up in the *vinter* in *Norvay* is every *vomen's vet* dream." The audience burst into laughter. And so did Blake and I. He squeezed my hand, and then when the lights went dark, he kissed me. There was no doubt in my mind that

Grandma's new show, *The Sexy Shmexy Book Club*, was going to be a big hit. And at the young age of eighty-six, she was going to be a huge star.

One Saturday morning in July after a delicious wake-up fuck, Blake told me to start packing my bags.

"Are we going away for the weekend?" I asked him, seated cross-legged on our bed and still bared to him. He was always still full of surprises.

"No." A wicked smile curled on his kissable lips.

I shot him a puzzled look. I could tell from the expression on his face he was up to something. "Can you at least give me a hint?"

He affectionately tugged my ponytail. "Does the word 'honeymoon' mean anything to you?"

Oh my God! My heart skipped a beat. We'd never taken one. The secret destination he'd teased me with had never materialized after my surgery. Work had gotten in the way. Excitement mixed with panic.

"But, Blake, I haven't cleared my schedule. I've got so much going on."

"Don't worry. Mrs. Cho and I took care of it. We canceled most of your meetings, and whatever there's left to do, Myles and Mrs. Cho can handle."

My heart began to race with excitement. "Blake, where are we going?"

He winked. "Not telling. It's still a surprise."

All I knew it was somewhere neither of us had ever been. My mind spun with possibilities.

"What should I bring along?"

He smirked. "Except for your passport, as little as possible. You won't be needing much."

A rush of hot tingles clustered between my legs. My eyes widened. Now, he really had me curious and excited.

"When are we leaving?"

"At noon. On my dad's private plane."

"Oh my God!" Teetering between elation and panic (the former winning), I flung my arms around him and kissed him fiercely. Our tongues danced passionately together.

He playfully tweaked my nipples and then slid a hand across my still heated wet cleft.

"Now, baby, I'm going to show you some of the activities our destination has to offer."

In a short hot breath, he was again fucking me senseless. I was so looking forward to our trip.

Chapter 25

Blake

We'd been two hours in the air, and it was time for my first surprise. To keep the surprise a surprise, I'd forced Jen to wear a blindfold. She'd reluctantly gone along with my demand.

"Blake, it feels like we're descending. Are we landing?"

I wished she could see my fiendish grin. "We have to make a little stop." *Just wait.*

"Why can't I take this blindfold off? I want to see where we are. Mexico?"

Impulsively, the little sneak reached for her face. I grabbed both her petite hands by their wrists in my large one.

"Uh, uh, uh, tiger. You're forcing me to do something I wasn't sure I wanted to do, but now I have to."

She turned her head toward me, her little scrunched up nose peeking out from the blindfold. Fuck, she was cute.

"Like what, Blake?"

Without saying a word, I dug my free hand into the

seat pocket where I'd stored my backup accessory. Then, in one smooth move, I pinned her hands behind her and snapped the metal devices around her slender wrists. The clink was like music to my ears.

"Blake! You've handcuffed me." She futilely tried to tear her hands apart, stretching the chain to its maximum pull. I stifled laughter.

"Baby, if you don't behave, I've got some ropes close by to bind those defiant little hands."

She grunted in frustration. I was enjoying every minute, and she was turning me on. While the plane descended, something ascended. It was time for Jen to make a little visit to *my* cockpit.

Writhing, she continued to tug at the cuffs to no avail. She let out a loud sigh. "Okay, Blake, if you promise to take these off me, I'll do anything you want."

Jeez. She was making it so easy peasy. With swiftness, I zipped down my fly. Out sprung big ole Mr. Burns, who was thoroughly enjoying the ride. I think by the expression on her face she knew what I wanted.

"Deal. Go down on me, tiger." Before she could utter a word, I shoved her head to my cock. In a heartbeat, her warm mouth was covering my wide crown.

"Suck on me, tiger. Suck on me hard. I want to come hard and fast." She nodded as I urged her mouth to descend, pressing on her scalp with the palm of my hand. She didn't need any more flight instruction from me; my tiger knew exactly what to do. Exactly how I liked it. I hissed and arched my spine as she slid her mouth down my rigid shaft, her tongue blazing a trail. My head pressed hard again the headrest. Holy shit. She was taking me to the hilt.

"Jesus, baby. That feels so fucking good." I could feel my mega-sized dick fill the hollows of her cheeks and the tip touch the base of her throat. Without prompting, she quickly returned to the crown, and then began bopping her head up and down my enormous erection with the ferocity and velocity of the tiger she was. My greedy cocky couldn't be happier. My balls were tightening and heat coiled through my groin. Just as the plane touched down, I came with a massive explosion of hot cum in her mouth. I yanked up her head by her ponytail and crashed my lips onto hers, rewarding her with a fierce, savage kiss. She moaned into my mouth as I tasted myself on her tongue.

"Baby, we've landed," I breathed, breaking the kiss. Holy fuck. What a landing! My cock was still flying high.

She ran the tip of her talented tongue around her lush lips, licking off the remains of my release.

"Blake. *Ahem.* The handcuffs…"

"Right." I lived by my father's words: a deal is a deal. Except there was one little problem. I couldn't find the fucking key.

Shitballs. This wasn't part of the plan. It was time for our next activity and this was so not going to look good.

Chapter 26

Jennifer

B lake was not a happy camper nor was I. He was driving like a maniac. A Chevy pickup no less. He'd asked Mrs. Cho to have someone pick us up when we landed, but somehow that had gotten lost in translation and instead she'd rented him a pickup truck. As mad as I was at him, I'd do anything to see my metrosexual hubby behind the wheel of this vehicle. *That* man in a pickup was like Batman in an RV.

"We need to find a Walmart," he grumbled.

"Why?" I gritted. I was still blindfolded and hand-cuffed, and I had no clue where we were except I knew it wasn't some romantic island. I waited impatiently for his response.

"So, I can buy a chainsaw and saw off your hand-cuffs."

Gah! The thought of Blake with a chainsaw sent a shiver down my spine. My life could be over. Mr. Born with a Silver Spoon in his Mouth was not exactly what I'd call handy. The only power tools he had any experience with were his tongue, his hands, and his cock.

"What about a locksmith?" My voice was urgent. "I'm sure one could make a key to unlock these damn things."

"That's a good idea, tiger."

"Why don't you take off my blindfold so I can keep my eyes peeled for one? And where the hell are we anyway?"

"That's not happening. And I'm not telling."

Two minutes later, Blake swerved off the road with a screech. My neck jerked painfully. I think I had whiplash. Horns were blasting at us from all directions.

"What the fuck are you doing, Blake? You're going to get us killed!"

"There's a Walmart straight ahead of us," he replied brightly.

Ten minutes later, Blake was leading me through the bustling mega-store. He had his fingers curled around my neck since holding one of my pinned back, cuffed hands was not an option. I could barely move my fingers. The fucking handcuffs were cutting off my circulation. Oh, was he going to pay for this. Big time!

I could only imagine what people thought as I stumbled through the store, trying to keep up with Blake's pace. Maybe they thought he was a bounty hunter who'd captured his prey. Or an undercover cop who was carting away a shoplifter. Well, at least with the blindfold, I couldn't see their bewildered expressions.

"Slow down," I yelled.

Without slowing down, Blake asked, "Where do you think we can find a locksmith? I've never been to a Walmart before."

Of course not. Mr. Beverly Hills had lived a life of privilege. The only department store he'd ever stepped foot in besides Saks was Neiman Marcus. Needless Markup as Libby and I often called it.

"The hardware department," I seethed.

"This store is so fucking big. That could be a mile away."

"Ask. Some. One."

Twenty long minutes later, because everyone Blake asked gave us different directions, we were back outside in the parking lot where a locksmith was stationed.

"Can you make us a key that will unlock these cuffs?" Blake asked him.

Standing with my back to the locksmith, I felt him take my hands in his and examine the cuffs.

"Sure, but it's going to take two hours."

Blake's voice grew louder by an octave and desperate. "What! We have to be somewhere important in a half hour."

Where the heck were we going? I was more curious than ever.

Blake continued. "Do you have a Plan B? I don't

care what it fucking costs."

The locksmith stretched my hands apart as far as they would go. He then splayed them on the counter. "Keep your fingers spread and don't move an inch."

BANG! My heart hammered. BANG again! Suddenly, my hands were free from one another. I massaged my wrists, not happy the cuffs were still circling them.

"Blake, how are we going to get these off?"

"We'll figure it out later. For now, think of them as jewelry."

Jewelry, my ass.

"How much do I owe you?" Blake asked my liberator.

"Forget it. It's on the house. Just tell me, was the sex good?"

"Yeah. It was fucking amazing."

Grimacing, I let Blake whisk me away. "How could you say that?"

"Lighten up, baby. You know you loved it."

Damn it, he was right.

We were back in the Chevy. I wasn't talking to Blake. Fuming, I kept my cuffed hands folded tightly across my chest. I'd had enough of this ruse. Blake's shenanigans. A short fifteen minutes later, we turned off the freeway and began winding down some city streets. At what must be a red light, I finally broke my silence.

"Now, where are we going?"

"You'll see in five minute."

Sure enough, five minutes later Blake parked the truck and helped me out of it.

"Watch your step." His arm around my shoulders, he ushered me up the curb.

"Can't I take this damn blindfold off?" I asked, inhaling the intoxicating scent of roses and honeysuckle evocative of my childhood. Maybe he was taking me to some romantic garden. Several unsteady steps later, I found myself crossing a threshold. A mélange of delectable aromas instantly wafted up my nose.

"Blake, where are we?" In a quick heartbeat, the blindfold slipped off, and in a stunned blink, I knew. I was home!

"SURPRISE!" shouted out the people nearest and dearest to me, all dressed in Sunday finery. My parents, Blake's parents, Gloria and Jaime Zander with their twins, Libby, Marcy and her twins, Vera and Steve Nichols and their son Joshua, Mrs. Cho and her family, my therapist, Dr. Williams, and, last but not least, Grandma with Luigi the tailor. Also gathered in the hallway were Father Murphy and some of my parents' closest friends. The people I'd grown up with. My jaw dropped to the floor. I was simply aghast.

"Blake, is this some kind of surprise party? My

birthday's not till October."

He smacked a kiss on my cheek "No, baby. It's a surprise wedding."

A wedding? "But—"

My mother, looking positively stunning in a damask silk suit that matched the color of her gray-blue eyes, broke out of the crowd and gave me hug before I could say another word.

"Come on, honey. Let's get you ready."

"But, Mom, I have nothing appropriate to wear."

Beaming, she took my hand. "Excuse us, everyone. But the mother of the bride has to get her little girl ready." I shot a glance at my handsome, smiling father who winked at me. Then, I let Mom lead me to the stairwell with my head turned, my eyes never losing contact with Blake's. A cocky, triumphant smile lit his face. Oh, my Blake! *That* man who never stopped surprising me. His love filled the room.

A few breathless moments later, I stepped foot into my bedroom. And yet another shocking surprise.

Chaz! "Darling, just say yes to the dress."

He was holding up the most beautiful gown I'd ever seen. I gasped, clapping a hand to my wide-open mouth.

"Do you like it, Jenny-Poo?"

"Oh my God, Chaz. It's gorgeous." Tears were brimming in my eyes as I beheld his breathtaking creation. It was the dress I'd always dreamed of. A sleeveless, ivory confection with layers of tulle and lace, tiny scattered pearls, and a sweetheart neckline. I knew in my heart every stitch was made with love. Oh my sweet Chaz!

I broke away from my mom and ran up to hug him. Tears were now free-falling down my face.

"Darling, you're going to crush the dress. Come on, let's get you dressed."

To my utter delight, my best friend Libby joined us, and a half hour later, the magnificent dress cinched my narrow waist and grazed the carpeted floor. It fit me to a tee. Beneath the gown, I was wearing delicate lace lingerie and thigh-high silk stockings from Paris. All courtesy of Gloria. And a pair of ivory satin heels with sparkly snowflake shoe clips, courtesy of Libby.

"Mom, was this your idea?" I asked as she and Libby fluffed the dress.

"No, my darling. It was all Blake's."

My heart melted.

"I just helped him orchestrate it. And I must tell you, dear, his mother was a saint and helped so much. She's an amazing woman."

I smiled. I was so happy Helen and Mom were bonding. That was important to me. And since the Hollywood wedding debacle, she'd grown closer to me and relinquished control over Blake's social life. I had a lot to learn from her.

Chaz broke into my thoughts. "Jenny-Poo, we're

not done yet." My eyes followed him as he pranced over to my closet and opened it. Hanging from the hook was an exquisite long lace veil. I recognized it immediately. It was the one Blake's grandma had worn in that photo I'd once admired.

"Grandma insisted you wear it," my mother said brightly as Chaz adjusted it over my head. It trailed along the carpet.

"Oh, Jen, you look like a princess," gushed Libby, who once again was going to be my maid of honor. "Take a look at yourself."

Grabbing my hand, she led me to a full-length standing mirror in the corner of my small room.

I let out a little gasp as I stared at my reflection. My mother stood behind me and I could see her eyes watering in the glass.

"Oh, my little girl."

I spun around and gave her another hug. "Oh, Mom. I love you so much."

And then, I hugged Libby and Chaz again.

"No tears!" chastised Chaz. "They'll ruin your complexion."

"One last thing, darling," said my mother, dipping her hand into the pocket of her suit jacket.

"What's that?" I asked, eyeing a scrap of blue lace that looked very old.

"Something borrowed. Something blue. It's the garter I wore when I married your father. It belonged to your late grandmother."

My Irish grandmother, Maeve. A woman I'd heard much about but had sadly never met. I was close to losing it as I lifted my gown. My mother held it up as I slid the treasured heirloom up my silk-clad leg. Her eyes wandered to my wrists.

"Honey, I meant to ask you, what are those unusual bracelets you're wearing?"

I glanced at the shiny cuffs as I continued to inch the garter up my leg.

On one, the words "My tiger" were engraved; on the other, "You. Are. Mine."

I replied to my mom. "Oh, just some jewelry Blake wanted me to wear for our nuptials."

My Blake! At this moment, there was no happier or luckier girl in the world than me.

Chapter 27

Blake

I'll never forget the expression on my tiger's face as she stepped into her backyard on the arm of her proud, beaming father. She stopped dead in her tracks and her jaw dropped to the snow-covered ground.

That's right...snow in July. With the help of my mother and her new party planner, Jeffrey, I had magically transformed the McCoys' backyard into a winter wonderland. A snow machine was making snow and a fine layer dusted the lawn. While Jen was getting ready, I'd helped my nephews and Vera's son, Josh, finish building the snowman. He looked just like the snowman Jen and I had built that first Christmas together. We were getting married under a *chuppah* covered with snow white flowers on the very spot where we'd created our snow angel. Mr. Snowman, wearing a black bowtie and tall hat, was sharing the best man spotlight with my bud, Jaime, who stood next to Libby, Jen's maid of honor. Seats had been arranged for our guests, who I'd flown in on the Conquest Broadcasting jet, and there was also a white baby grand piano. Sitting at it was Roberta Flack herself—yes, I'd flown her in—playing and singing our song.

As the songstress tenderly sang "The First Time Ever I Saw Your Face," my cock flexed and my heart melted as I beheld my beautiful bride, her eyes glistening with joyous tears. The earth moved beneath my feet as she slowly approached me, her gaze never leaving mine. I was giving her the wedding she always wanted. The wedding she deserved. The wedding we would remember forever.

Mr. Peace, Love, and Happiness was officiating. Yup, Reverend Dooby. Under a slightly overcast sky, I took my tiger in my arms, and we exchanged our vows. To put each other's needs before our own and to never stop loving each other in good times or bad times. She recited a sonnet while I recited a poem I'd composed. With snowflakes dancing all around us, I lifted her veil and tugged her head back by her ponytail. I held that pretty face in my gaze for a long hot beat and then kissed her the way I had the first time. That very first time I'd seen her face and my life had changed forever. As my mouth consumed hers in a passionate, all-consuming kiss, the sun broke through the clouds. Our snow angel was watching.

Chapter 28

Jennifer

That man.

As I stood on the balcony of the private villa Blake had rented and watched the sun set into the cerulean Tahitian sea, I couldn't stop reliving my wedding. They say the third time's a charm, but I would marry *that* man again and again. The beautiful memories whirled around in my head as the soft sound of the surf resounded in my ears.

Blake had given me the wedding every girl dreamed of. A celebration of love shared by the special people in our lives. I recited the Shakespearean sonnet and he composed a poem. Just for me. Okay, so he stole the first line from another Blake—"Tiger, tiger, burning bright"—but the rest of it was totally original. And so, so moving. The words were still dancing in my head. He compared me to a star and told me he loved me close up and from afar. And then he said I gave him direction and guiding light. "Until death do us part. My heart is yours; yours mine whatever our plight." He would totally always love me.

And then we said our "I do's" and he kissed me deeply, passionately. Just like that very first kiss that had started it all. When I danced in his arms to Roberta Flack's soulful rendition of "For the First Time in Forever" from my favorite movie, *Frozen*, my heart swelled with happiness, and then I danced in the arms of my dad to the singer's moving rendition of "The Wind Beneath My Wings." Yes, my other forever hero. I melted in his arms too.

Both my dad and Blake's gave awesome speeches that brought laughter as well as tears. And heartfelt, often hilarious toasts abounded. Every one had an outrageous story to tell about Blake. My man was a very naughty boy. And I loved him all the more for it. One, in particular, tickled my heart. Jaime's. He ended it by toasting me: "To the woman who taught Blake Burns that his cock is connected to his heart." Everyone roared with laughter while a blushing Blake kissed me again.

I got a little drunk and sang "Roar" to Blake while Roberta belted the piano. Soon after, Libby caught my bouquet of fresh flowers picked right from our back-yard, and Chaz caught my garter. But there was going to be another wedding before theirs. Over champagne and my mom's delicious homemade buttercream wedding cake, Grandma made a toast to her Blakela and Bubala *shtupping* in good health forever and then an announcement. She and Luigi were stopping off in

Vegas on their way back to LA and getting married *shmarried*. Cheers erupted! YAY for Grandma!

After Grandma's announcement, Blake stole me away from the festivities, and we fucked our brains out in my childhood bedroom; the dress stayed put, and under the layers of tulle and lace, I came a multitude of glorious times.

Soon afterward, we reboarded the private plane. Though no longer blindfolded, I still had no idea where we were going. Blake still refused to tell me. And it was dark. Yet had it been daylight, I still wouldn't know because I didn't spend much time gazing out the window. My face was either buried between Blake's thighs or hovering over a chair cushion while he rammed into me from behind. And in between fucking our brains out, I slept dreamily in his arms in an in-flight bed made for royalty.

I returned to the moment. As the South Seas sun disappeared into ocean like a ball of fire, a warm breath tickled my neck and a sultry voice swept me out of my delicious memories. Blake. My husband.

"Merry Christmas, baby."

I felt something hard and cold drape around my neck. I looked down and gasped. Circling my throat was a strand of lustrous beads that hung down past my breasts. They were iridescent green—almost the color of my eyes—and had a pavé diamond clasp. I spun around. Leaning against the balcony, I soaked in my breathtaking man. Shirtless, he was wearing a pair of white sweats that hung sexily low on his hips and skimmed his perfect pelvic V. The tropical breeze ruffled his tousled hair and that dazzling smile lit his gorgeous sun-kissed face. I cupped my palms over his broad sculpted shoulders and searched his ocean-blue eyes.

"Blake, Christmas is not for another five months. What is this?" Whatever this exquisite necklace was, it was mega-expensive.

He adjusted the strand. "They're Tahitian peacock green pearls—the rarest of all. I was going to give them to you last Christmas but—"

His voice trailed off, but before he could say another word, I crushed my lips against his. "Oh Blake, they're so beautiful. I love you so much," I gushed after breaking away.

With a yank of a string, he pulled off my bikini top. My breasts quivered under his lustful gaze. Grasping the rope of pearls, he began to slowly circle them around my nipples. At the erotic, cold touch of them, my buds hardened, and a hot rush of tingles blossomed in my core. Goose bumps spread across my flesh while wetness pooled between my legs.

"I want a proper thank you, *Mrs.* Burns," he purred, now squeezing together my breasts with the strand. My eyes shot down. A big bulge dominated his sweats. Obviously, the pearls were multi-functional. My new piece of jewelry was his new toy.

As his mouth melted into mine, I slid down his sweats and then my bikini bottom. Fisting his wondrous cock, I glided it inside me.

"That's better." He winked as he began to pound me.

By the following morning, his cock had been many places. And so had my pearls.

Mrs. Burns had a lot to look forward to. Our honeymoon had just begun.

Epilogue

Blake

Christmas, Five Years Later

"Merry Christmas, tiger," I said brightly after planting a loud wake-up kiss on my wife's warm lips. My gaze stayed on her as she fluttered opened her eyelids. She looked like an angel, her mouth parted slightly, her porcelain skin flawless, her lustrous hair fanned out like wings, and her eyes dreamy.

She smiled. "Merry Christmas, baby."

After five years of marriage, Jen had not converted to Judaism. But she had taken some courses at our family synagogue and was even studying Hebrew so she could read the prayers with me. And she'd become, thanks to Grandma's mentoring, a wonderful Jewish cook—even able to make a Chanukah brisket as good as hers. The arrangement we had worked for both of us, and best of all, we celebrated all the holidays we'd each grown up with. I had to admit Christmas was my favorite.

Jen sat up slowly. Her still sleepy eyes glanced

down at my hand. "What's that you're holding?"

A fiendish grin spread across my face. "It's one of your Christmas presents," I replied, handing her the small gift-wrapped box. A sparkling green bow topped the shiny red paper.

Carefully, she plucked off the bow and then tore off the wrapping. Excitement danced in her eyes as she beheld the black velvet box beneath.

"Come on, open it," I urged. I couldn't wait to see the expression on her face. This was a good one. God's former gift to women was a genius when it came to giving gifts. Call me the gift that keeps on giving.

"Okay," she murmured, snapping open the lid. Her eyes grew wide as she stared at the iridescent pink ring.

"Is this a piece of jewelry?" she asked, her tone perplexed. She lifted the ring out of the box and put it on her middle finger. I must say it went very nicely with the pink tourmaline heart-pendant necklace I'd given her our very first Christmas together. Except it was a little big. Okay very big. That's because it was made for something super big. My cock.

I slipped the ring off her finger. "Baby, it's a toy for you. A piece of jewelry for *me*. A cock ring."

Her brows shot up. "A cock ring?"

Despite my giving her a battery-operated sex toy every Christmas (my little tradition), she was still so naïve it was adorable. I couldn't help but laugh. "Yeah, it's going to make me bigger and more powerful."

"But, Blake, you don't need to be any bigger or more powerful."

"Trust me, baby, every man can use a little extra something. And you're just going to love the attached vibrating heart bullet."

I'd done a lot of research looking for the perfect battery-operated accessory. Trust me, I was not the one-size-fits-all type of guy. The cock ring I'd finally found was made of a soft, stretchy material. It could expand as I expanded. Nice—totally worth the exorbitant price unless it was false advertising. I shoved the duvet down and there he was—Mr. Burns—commando and at attention, ready for playtime in our favorite playground. I'd woken up, as usual, with a mighty boner.

"Put the ring on me, tiger."

Wordlessly, she took the ring from me and slipped it over my enormous erection. Her innocent green eyes met mine, begging for further instruction.

"Now slide it down to the base."

Responsively, she edged it down with her deft fingers until it was right where I wanted it. It felt good—not too loose, not too tight. I flicked on the vibrator. The soft buzz sounded in my ears as I sat back on my elbows and flexed my knees.

"Sit on me, baby, facing the mirror." In my extensive research, I'd learned that reverse cowgirl was the ideal position for maximizing the benefits of this little toy. It happened to be one of our favorite positions. And this magical toy was only going to make it better.

Guiding my cock into her, she did as bid. I had a bird's eye view of her sweet ass and the beautiful curve of her back. Man, that delicious pair of dimples where the two met was so damn sexy. They fucking turned me on.

I began to thrust in and out of her, picking up speed with each long, hard stroke. I could feel my cock getting bigger, as if that was possible, swelling to epic proportions. A super-erection! My breathing grew shallow and I was working up a sweat. My buzzing cock was making me buzz everywhere. Jen reached her hands back and placed them firmly on my hipbones to hold on. This was one hell of a ride.

"Oh Blake," she cried out, arching back her head. "This is amazing."

Watching the two of us fuck in the mirror, I couldn't agree more. Besides being so hot and wet, she was taking my cock to the hilt. I felt the tip pounding her womb with each powerful thrust—for sure hitting her magic spot—while the vibrating bullet attachment stimulated her clit. I always went many rounds, but my, I meant *her,* new toy was sustaining my erection beyond belief. Holy shit! This toy was the bomb. Seriously, I'd give it ten stars on Amazon if I could. As my tiger began to whimper on the brink of an epic orgasm, a loud knock-knock-knock sounded at the door. *Shit.*

"Mommy, Daddy! Wakey up! I wanna see if Santa came and left me *pwesents.*"

The other love of my life. Our adorable three-and-a-half-year-old...Leo. My heart melted at the sound of his sweet little raspy voice.

"Coming, sweetie pie," shouted Jennifer. "And so is Daddy." Oh, fuck were we. On the next hard thrust, she convulsed all around me while I exploded like a stick of dynamite. Playtime was over. Time to *unbig* myself. Next activity. I couldn't wait to open presents under our Christmas tree. To see my little man's expression as he unwrapped his, and that of my tiger when she saw what I had in store for her. *Ho! Ho! Ho!*

Our majestic Christmas tree sat in the bay window of our large living room. Almost ceiling high, it was decorated with many of the ornaments Jennifer had collected as a child. We'd picked out the tree together with Leo and had decorated it over cookies and hot chocolate. Leo loved helping hang the ornaments as much as he loved helping light our Chanukah candles.

Right after Leo—named after my grandpa, Leonard—was born, I sold my Wilshire Corridor condo and found our dream house right on the beautiful, coveted street across from the Santa Monica Stairs where Jen and I worked out every weekend. While it was hardly the size of my parents' palatial estate (something neither Jen nor I wanted), it was stately and spacious and reminded Jennifer of some of the large houses in Boise she'd grown up around. There was a big grassy backyard, a gated pool, and a guest house where Jen's parents stayed whenever they visited. Which was often. In fact, they were occupying it right now. Barely dawn, I was sure they'd be here later in the morning to share our Christmas festivities. Most Christmases, we traveled to Boise and Sun Valley, but this time, we needed to stay close to home. Just in case...So, Jen's parents, never wanting to miss a Christmas with their beloved grandson, came to LA.

"Oh boy, Daddy! Looky at what Santa got me!" Leo squealed as he tore apart a huge box wrapped with whimsical snowman paper and a big bow. He could barely hold the package in his little hands. "Combat Wombats!"

"Wow!" I winked. "You must have been a really good boy." Yours truly, Santa, had cleaned out the entire section of these bestselling toys. I'd bought him everything from action figures to the motorized Wombatmobile, which he could actually sit in and drive down the street.

Leo smiled broadly, his two cute dimples bracketing his mouth just like mine. "Will you play with me, Daddy?"

God, I loved that last word. And the way he said it.

DAD-dee. And I loved being *that* man. I told him for sure after breakfast. Leo gleefully opened the rest of his presents—okay, I was spoiling the kid, but what the hell—and then Jennifer and I exchanged ours. She handed me mine first. It was monstrous and quite heavy. I carefully tore apart the exquisite metallic wrapping. At the sight of what was beneath, my eyes grew wide and my heart smiled. It was a framed oil portrait of Leo and me. I fucking loved it.

"Tiger, I love it," I said, forcing myself not to say the f-word in front of Leo. I smacked my lips against hers. Leo was too busy playing with his new toys to notice.

Jen smiled warmly and brushed her hand through my hair. "I want you to hang it in your new office."

That was a great idea. At the age of thirty-five, I was now the head of Conquest Broadcasting. I'd inherited my retired father's expansive top floor office suite and had more wall space than I knew what do with. I knew exactly where I was going to hang it. Right by the entrance so I could look at it all day. I gently set the painting down on the antique rug. Now, it was my turn to give Jen her present. I handed her a small Christmassy shopping bag to which I'd attached a large SpongeBob "Merry Christmas" balloon.

"I know it doesn't look like much." My voice trailed off as she took the bag from me and removed a bright red eight by ten envelope. My eyes stayed fixed on her as she unfastened it and slipped out a single sheet of paper. Her green eyes widened and her jaw dropped to the floor as she read the announcement. The paper shook in her trembling hands.

"Oh my God, Blake. You bought back Peanuts?"

Peanuts was the children's network she'd hoped to work at when she was first hired by my father, but he'd sold it just before she came on board. Jen had always dreamed of working in children's programming but was forced to work for the porn channel I headed up. SIN-TV. What a fine job she had done. With passion and perseverance, she'd created a mega-successful women's erotica channel, MY SIN-TV. But now, it was time for her to move on. And to have a family-friendly career. I'd closed the top secret deal only yesterday. Peanuts was officially now once again part of the Conquest Broadcasting media family. And it was going to be part of our little family too.

I held Jen's stunned face in my gaze. "And, tiger, you're going to run it. Get used to your new title: President, Peanuts TV."

She gasped. A hand flew to her gaping mouth. Finally, she found her voice. A stammer. "B-but, who's going to run MY SIN-TV?"

"Don't worry about it, baby. I'm promoting Myles." Myles Harding was my gay head of programming for SIN-TV, but I'd learned he'd been dying to work for our women's counterpart. It was all going to work out perfectly. My tiger was finally going to have the chance to live out her dream and create her very own Sponge-Bob. And a lineup of programs that would make me proud—and our children elated. She was going to be *our* superhero. With my thumb, I tilted up her chin.

"Do you like your present, tiger?"

A huge smile adorned her face. "Oh, Blake, it's the best Christmas gift ever." She flung her arms around me and crushed her lips against mine. Our tongues danced joyously, and I became lost in our passionate embrace. A little voice broke us apart.

"Mommy, I'm *hungwee.*"

Jen flushed with embarrassment and excused herself to make breakfast.

While she toiled in the kitchen, Leo and I retreated to the adjacent family room where we cuddled together on the comfy over-stuffed couch. With Leo snug on my lap, I picked up the remote and clicked on the big screen TV facing us. Wouldn't you know it...the SpongeBob Christmas episode was on—the very one I'd watched with Jen at her parents' house—our fateful first Christmas together. Leo loved SpongeBob as much as Jen and I did. As was our ritual, the two of us sang the silly opening credits song together at the top of our lungs, shouting out SpongeBob SquarePants each time it was mentioned.

The episode began, and Leo instantly broke out into a cluster of giggles at one of SpongeBob's hilariously endearing antics. His sweet laughter was contagious. Ruffling my little man's unruly dark hair, I joined him.

My little cub. He was the spitting image of me. Except he had Jen's incredible long-lashed green eyes. Every time I looked into them, I recalled the first time I set my eyes on Jen's—the day I interviewed her for a job at SIN-TV. And how they'd mesmerized me and reduced me to a spluttering mess.

Grandma had said, "Blakela, you're gonna get *vun* just like you." She was right, and she was wrong.

I was a holy terror as a child. But not, my Leo. I knew every parent boasted their kid's the best kid in the world. But let me tell you, mine was. He'd been the perfect baby. Slept the night and was all smiles. And now he was the sweetest, smartest toddler in the world. Already potty trained. Number one in his pre-school. And definitely, the most popular kid too. Little girls fawned all over him. This kid was born a player. On the playground, he was already breaking lots of shovels *and* hearts. I was going to have to teach him a thing or two about love when he got older.

Leo was the perfect name for him. Born in July, he was definitely a lion. He ruled the playground; he ruled our lives. He roared when he cried; he roared when he laughed. His middle name was Ness, which meant miracle in Hebrew and indeed he was. A gift from God. Following Jen's hysterectomy, Marcy had told us since Jen had been spared an ovary, she could still produce quality eggs. The problem was she couldn't carry a child. Marcy turned us on to one of her colleagues—a top fertility doctor. And simultaneously introduced us to a very special surrogate who wanted to carry our child. On the very first attempt, one of my little swimmers fertilized one of Jen's eggs via IVF—in vitro fertilization. The embryo was transferred to our surrogate and nine months later, we were a family.

Halfway through the cartoon, the tantalizing aroma of pancakes and sausage drifted in the air. I was famished.

Just as the episode wrapped up, Jen called out, "Guys, breakfast is ready."

I set my little man on the floor. "C'mon, I'll race you to the kitchen."

Leo's eyes lit up. It was another one of our rituals. I always let him win. I was raising him—or should I say, we were raising him to be a winner just the way my parents raised me. And instilling in him the value of going after what you want in life. So far, that was a lot of toys, cookies, and goodnight stories.

"Mommy, I beat Daddy again," boasted Leo as he energetically ran into the large kitchen on his little pajama-clad legs.

A big smile beamed on Jen's animated face as I feigned exhaustion with pants. What an actor I was! The one thing I never had to act out was climaxing with my tiger. Fortunately, Leo's room was far away enough from ours so my tiger could still roar my name. And man, did she.

With breakfast already on the table, Jen swept Leo into her arms and smothered him with kisses. "That's awesome, my sweetness."

I eyed them proudly. Happiness filled every crevice of my body. I always knew my Jen would make a great mother and she was. And soon, there would be another cub to add to our den.

Joining them at the kitchen table, I couldn't wait to dig into breakfast. I was ravenous. I reached for the bottle of maple syrup on the lazy Susan, and as I doused my sausage with it, my eyes met Jen's. Ever since that breakfast over five years ago at Jaime and Gloria's beach house, maple syrup made me horny as hell. It had the same effect on Jen. We read each other's eyes. Yup, she was thinking what I was thinking. Right after breakfast, we'd have our live-in nanny take Leo for a ride in his new Wombatmobile down the street while we fucked our brains out and sent each other orbiting.

As Jen poured coffee from the French press into my mug, her cell phone, charging on the counter, rang. Her signature ringtone—the melody of Roberta Flack's "The First Time Ever I Saw Your Face"—played. Setting the glass vestibule down, she leapt up from her seat and sprinted to the phone. My gaze stayed riveted on her great ass and taut legs that had become shapelier and more muscular from doing the Santa Monica Stairs with me regularly. Her ponytail bounced with her sprite gait.

Putting the phone to her ear, her eyes grew as wide as saucers. "Oh my God," I overheard her say. "I'll be right there." She ended the call.

"Baby, what's going on?"

"Marcy's at Cedars."

"Holy shit!" *Fuck.* I didn't mean to curse in front of my son. I just couldn't help it.

"I'm heading over. Get there as soon as you can."

Not bothering to change out of her sweats, Jen grabbed her car keys. She brushed by the table, giving Leo and me each a big kiss, and dashed out the door.

It was time to break out another expensive box of Cuban cigars.

Jennifer

Libby wasn't supposed to give birth for another two weeks. Her water had broken early, and when I arrived at Cedars, she was already in the delivery room. Marcy was hovering over her, in green scrubs and a facemask, similar to the ones I was forced to put on. A team of nurses surrounded them.

Libby was plopped up against a mountain of pillows, clad in a pink hospital gown, her knees bent and splayed.

"Lib!" I shouted out, running up to her side.

My bestie smiled faintly and managed to wave to me.

"Breathe," Marcy commanded.

"How's she doing?" I asked Blake's sister, my voice laden with worry.

"Great."

Libby blew out short, sharp breaths. Pants.

I squeezed her hand. Her fiery red curls were matted to her sweat-laced face.

"Push," ordered Marcy.

"Fuck," grunted Libby as she did as asked. Her freckled face turned as red as her hair.

"Are you in pain?" My voice was shaky.

Breathing as instructed, she shook her head. Her extended belly rose up and down.

Libby was giving birth to our second child.

Yes, my best friend in the world, now happily married to a great guy and the mother of twins (another story!), had offered to be our surrogate after I told her Marcy, our first surrogate, felt our chances for a successful pregnancy would be better with a younger woman.

Choosing not to remarry though she was contently involved with an older, respected doctor, Marcy was now close to forty-five. She was the best sister-in-law in the world. That day in her office two months after my surgery, she gave Blake and me a priceless wedding present. The gift of life. *A family.* As I watched Libby labor, I flashed back to that moment and then to the epic birth of Leo. After a long struggle, he came out roaring like a lion.

A shriek from Libby pierced the air and cut into my thoughts. My already frenetic heartbeat sped up.

"One more push!" urged Marcy.

My unblinking eyes stayed glued on my best friend as she grunted a loud breath, tears streaming down her scrunched up face, and then they widened as a tiny dark-haired head emerged between her bent legs. I bit down hard on my bottom lip as she continued to grunt and push out the tiny life form with Marcy's gloved hands gently guiding it into the world.

The next thing I knew, the unmistakable wails of a newborn were filling my ears.

With a heavy sigh of relief, Libby fell back against the pillows. I hugged her.

"Lib, you did it!"

"We did it!" Libby beamed, her voice strong for a woman who'd just given birth.

Oh, my Lib! *Always there for me!* My eyes shifted to Marcy.

Smiling beneath her mask, she cradled the tiny baby in her arms while two of the nurses cleaned her up and then swaddled her in a soft pink blanket.

"Congratulations!" they said in unison as they transferred her into my arms.

Breathless and wordless, I gazed down at our little girl. Our miracle. Our beautiful miracle. I couldn't wait for Blake to meet her.

Blake

It took all I had not to drive like a madman. Thank fucking God, the streets were empty. A rarity for LA but typical for Christmas Day. Jen's father was seated beside me in the Range Rover (our family car), and in the backseat, Leo was strapped into his car seat with Mrs. McCoy planted on the adjacent cream leather seat. My heart was in my throat and beating a mile a minute. "Santa Claus is Coming to Town" was blasting on the radio, and Leo was singing along in his adorable pitch-perfect voice. Oh, yeah, Santa had come. That's for sure. But I just didn't expect *this* present today of all days. The plans we had for later were scrapped—to see an animated movie and then go to Chinatown with my parents, Grandma, and Luigi. I tried calling Jen. No answer. Clenching the steering wheel and my teeth, I could hear my palpitating heart in my ear and feel it beat in my throat. Libby was way early and I was fucking freaking.

Arriving at Cedars, I left the car with the VIP valet,

and with Leo riding me piggyback, I dashed into the hospital. The McCoys trailed close behind us, fit enough to keep up with me.

"Daddy, why we go to the hospital?" Leo breathed into my ear. "I no fall down."

Besides being born here, he'd been to Cedars once before—the emergency room—when he'd fallen off our backyard jungle gym and cut open his chin. My poor little man needed three stitches. While he was as brave as the lion he was, yours truly, Mr. Cowardly, almost needed smelling salts to get through the ordeal.

"Why, Daddy?" my son asked again.

"It's a surprise," I said breathlessly. *And it better be a good one.*

"Tell me, Daddy, what it is," Leo begged.

Before I could respond, my cell phone rang. My breath hitched as I picked it up on the first ring. Jen!

Thank you, Jesus. Now, I just had to find Room 3020.

Jennifer

"Oh honey, she looks just like you!" said my teary-eyed mother, who was gathered around me along with my elated father, Blake, and Leo. I was seated in a comfortable armchair, our newborn in my arms. Libby, believe it or not, had already rebounded from the record-fast delivery and was taking a stroll through the maternity ward to give us some alone time with the new addition to our family.

"An Irish beauty!" chimed in my proud dad.

I glanced down at her. Indeed, she was with her milky skin, tuft of ebony hair, and long-lashed blue-green eyes. Just fed, her rosebud lips pursed with contentment. I gently kissed the top of her silky scalp and inhaled her intoxicating newborn scent. Lifting my head, my eyes met Blake's glistening blue orbs. Standing motionless, he was a cross between a zombie and a god.

"Here, Blake. Hold her." I stood up and carefully transferred our little bundle of love into his strong manly arms.

"Hi, princess," he said softly, the awed expression on his face melting my heart.

Never taking his eyes off her, he slowly lowered himself to the armchair. Leo was eye-level with the baby.

"Say hi to your sister, Maeve, my little man."

Maeve. Blake and I had chosen that name together. An homage to my late grandmother, it meant "the cause of great joy" and indeed she was. The best Christmas present ever.

Staring at his sister, Leo asked, "Where did she come from, Daddy? Don't babies come from mommies' tummies?"

A smile lit Blake's lips. "She's magic. Just like you."

Puzzled, adorable Leo cocked his head. "Me abracadabra?"

Blake chuckled. "One day when you're a big boy, I'll teach you the trick."

Leo reciprocated with a big dimpled smile and then unexpectedly, he kissed our newborn on her forehead. My beaming parents hovered over them.

I quickly snapped a photo with my iPhone. And then I blinked my eyes like the shutter of a camera lens and took a mental snapshot of this magnificent moment that would stay in my mind forever. The album of life.

Overwhelmed with emotion, I continued to gaze at Blake—*that* man with whom I'd shared this incredible journey. Life, I'd learned, is not a fait accompli. A simple dare can change the course of everything…take you down a miraculous road you thought you'd never travel. A road to happiness and true love.

As Blake lovingly held our little girl with our precious little boy beside him, my heart exploded. My body tingled from my head to my toes. And tears welled up in my eyes. Blake had given me more than happiness. He'd given *me* joy. An emotion so powerful it couldn't be put into words.

I looked forward to the next leg of our journey. To raising our children and growing old together. In my heart, I knew Leo would one day grow up to be *that* special man to a wonderful woman and our little princess would find her own *that* man to love and protect her. Like I had with Blake Burns.

My husband. My lover. The father of our children. My hero.

Oh, how I love *that* man.

THE END

…well, almost…

A LETTER FROM BLAKE

Hey there all you beautiful and sexy readers~

Come on. You know me by now. There's no way I was going to let my tiger get the last word in as much as I love her. I am, after all, that good-looking guy on the cover, the one who inspired this story.

I just want to thank you for sharing our adventure. It was some rollercoaster ride, huh? A couple of times we almost fell off. And no way could I have saved her. But there's something mightier than a superhero. Another four-letter F-word. *Fate.* They say fate's a bitch, but I'm glad she is because Jen and I ended up together.

My sister told me Jen's made me a better person. She's right. My tiger has. Remember that guy at the beginning who thought with his cock? Well, I've got to admit I still do, but like my pal, Jaime Zander, said at our wedding, I learned my cock is connected to my heart. My cock has an appetite but my heart hungers too. I fuck hard. I love harder.

It's sometimes hard to believe the player you once knew is now the family guy. Man, if I'd only known what it's like to hold a newborn in my arms, I would have had kids a lot sooner, but I had to wait for the right woman. Jen will tell you I went to heaven and back.

And the first time my little cubs smiled at me, my heart melted like an M&M in my mouth.

Just like my father, I'm damn good at my new job though I'll confess Mr. Gift Who Keeps Giving spoils those two beautiful kids. I'm also a little over protective. Okay, so I'm over the top in that department. Being a parent brings out the superhero in me. Trust me, God fucking help the man who lays hands on my princess—even worse, who lays her. He'd better have a safe place to hide.

Yup, Jen turned me into a man I can be proud of. A loving, loyal husband, father, friend, and lover. And she turned me into a poet too. I've come a long way since copying Hallmark cards and writing those dumbass limericks. Okay, so my poetry isn't going to win a Pulitzer, but I've got to say it's pretty darn good.

They say the third time's a charm. And it is. After our third wedding, we got our happily every after. We still have our little ups and downs—what marriage doesn't?—but it's perfectly imperfect. I will love Jen for richer, for poorer (fat chance), in sickness and in health until death do us part. My tiger's stuck with me forever. I will always be *that* man.

Thank you for rooting for us. Putting up with us. (Yeah, I know you wanted to slap us more than a couple of times.) And sharing our story.

I.T.A.L.Y.~ xo Blake

ACKNOWLEDGMENTS

As I wrote the two little words, "The End," tears filled my eyes. It was so hard to say good-bye to *THAT MAN*—Blake Burns. What a journey this has been! I have so many people to thank.

Deep breath! This is going to be long and I hope don't forget anyone.

Usually, I thank them last, but this time they're going first. My family. Thank you for putting up with me while I wrote and edited this epic story over the past year. My sweet girls, I'm sorry for all the crappy meals, the number of times I growled, "Leave me alone," and all the times I told you to Uber home. A special shout out goes to my husband—my very own *that* man who picked up much of the mommy slack while I slaved at my computer. By the way, he's convinced he's Blake. I say wishful thinking, or should I say I wish. Regardless, thank you, babe, for your love and support—and for admittedly giving me some of my best Blake lines.

My second heartfelt round of thanks goes to my amazing beta readers. Across the series, they include in alphabetical order: Kelly Butterfield, Michelle Coddington, Amber Lynn Escalera, Kashunna Fly, Kellie Fox, Alma Garcia, Tracy "Sunshine" Graver, Gloria Herrera, Wanda Kather, Cindy Meyer, Kim Pinard

Newsome, Jen Oreto, Sheena Reid, Jasmine Roman, Jenn Moshe Silverstein, Karen Silverstein, and Jeanette Sinfield. I'm blessed to have the best betas in the whole wide world. You are all so smart, funny, and insightful, and didn't hold back for better or for worse. You have become more than betas; you have become my friends.

Arianne Richmonde and Adriane Leigh, my two best writer friends (my BWF's) also deserve big hugs. Thank you for reading *THAT MAN* and for all your great suggestions. Most of all, thank you for keeping me sane and getting me through the many times I thought I could never write another word or finish. Trust me, only fellow authors understand the formidable challenge of writing a book, let alone a five-part series. I don't know what I would have done without my besties, who listened to my rants as well as shared many laughs and glasses of wine.

Many of you may remember that *THAT MAN 1* first appeared in *Love and Laughter,* a romantic comedy anthology. I want to thank Zirconia Publishing and all the wonderful, hardworking authors who participated in that anthology and worked painstakingly together to make it a *USA Today* bestseller. These amazing ladies and a gent include Abi Aiken, Harper Ashe, Dez Burke, Adriana Hunter, Arianne Richmonde, Aubrey Rose, Marian Tee, and Terry Towers. Love to you all.

The success of the *THAT MAN* series can also be attributed to the many hardworking bloggers who embraced Blake Burns and wrote wonderful reviews that helped spread the word. A special thanks to Mary Tatar of Love Between the Sheets Promotions who spearheaded my blog tours as well as wrote some of my favorite reviews. There are so many bloggers to thank, but I want to single out a few who have been with me throughout my writing career and who have gone out of their way to put *THAT MAN* in front of readers. They include in no particular order: Jen Oreto/*Book Avenue Reviews,* Becky Barney/*The Fairest of All,* Ellen Widom/*The Book Bellas*, Selene Cabadas/*Sassy Girl Reviews*, Gloria Herrera/*As You Like it Reviews*, Desirae Shie/*Books, Chocolate, and Lipgloss*, Jennifer Noe/*The Book Blog*, Mags Pereira and Jewelz Fowler/*SMI Book Club*, Lynn Booth/*Chasing Orion's Rouge Odyssey*, Sheeba Ellison/*Bedtime Reviews*, Lorraine Masterson/*Rusty's Reading*, Gillian Gybras/ *A is for Alpha B is for Books*, Cindy Meyer and Deborah Presley /*The Book Enthusiast*, Jennifer McCoy/*SubClub Books*, Lisa Pantano Kane and Jennifer Skewes/ *Three Chicks and Their Books*, Nicole Scott/ *My Book Filled Life*, and Susan Harwood/*Wicked Women Promotions*, who has also hosted my fab Facebook Release Day parties.

I would be remiss not to thank one other entity—the amazing newsletter, *Book Bub.* I feel so blessed that you chose *THAT MAN 1* as one of your Free Books of the Day. Thanks to that promotion, the story of Blake and his tiger touched the hearts of countless readers and made *THAT MAN* an international bestseller.

The team that ultimately brings my books to fruition merits a big shout out. Thank you, Paul Salvette/BB eBooks for flawlessly formatting both my e-books and paperbacks and putting up with all my crazy revisions; Arijana Karcic /Cover It! Designs for all the glorious covers and my Facebook banner, and Karen Lawson for proofing my manuscripts and for making me laugh with your snarky comments. I am also beholden to "my Blue Ranger," for creating beta mobiFiles and to my beloved fan and super-talented friend, Kellie Fox, who magically creates all those fabulous panty-melting graphics you see on my Facebook page. I also want to acknowledge my amazing PA, Alma Garcia, who helps techno-challenged me in so many ways, and my mega-fan, Cathy Dotson Guadagnino, who cheers me on constantly. And I should mention, a big kiss goes to Robert Reider for being my gorgeous cover model and to his delightful mother Klara, who reached out to me and has become a lovely friend.

Almost last but not least, I want to thank all my readers who have embraced *THAT MAN* and fallen in love, like me, with Blake Burns. Had it not been for your support and encouragement, I wouldn't have written Blake and Jen's wedding story. A special shout-out goes to those who have written heartfelt reviews, sent me heartwarming emails, and commented or PM'd me on Facebook. Your kind, often beautiful words always brighten my day and make me persevere. My love to all of you; you are the reason I write.

Finally, I want to thank my father-in-law, aka "Mr. I. Wackit," and my open-minded mom for believing in me and being proud of me. And thank you, Daddy, too, for always being there for me. So much of your *menschiness* inspired Blake. I miss you and will always love you. *Sniff*

Okay. I did it! I hope I got everyone! As for me, I'm back to writing 24/7. Next up is *Gloria's Forever*, a novella, coming out in March 2015. Then, in April 2015, I will be releasing a panty-melting brand new series—*Unforgettable*. Just like Blake Burns, my new sexy as sin hero, Brandon Taylor, will make you laugh, cry, and swoon. And best of all Blake and the entire *THAT MAN* gang, including Grandma, will be featured! Meanwhile, I hope you'll enjoy Grandma's famous matzo ball soup in more ways than one; the secret recipe follows. In between rolling and sucking those balls, be sure to sign up for my newsletter to stay abreast of my new releases and sales. Here's the link: http://eepurl.com/N3AXb.

To all my Belles, thank you again from the bottom of my heart for your love and support. It means the world to me.

MWAH! ~ Nelle ♥

GRANDMA'S FAMOUS MATZO BALL SOUP
(Serves 6)

Bubalas, trust me, the *vay* to a man's heart—and his *shmekel*—is through his stomach. Make him my delicious matzo ball soup and you'll be *shtupping* for hours. *Zei gezunt!* Enjoy!

INGREDIENTS

CHICKEN STOCK
- 1 4-5-lb chicken (preferably Kosher), cut into 8 pieces
- 1 pound chicken wings, necks, and/or backs
- 2 large yellow onions, unpeeled, quartered
- 6 celery stalks, cut into 1" pieces
- 4 large carrots, peeled, cut into 1" pieces
- 1 large parsnip, peeled, cut into 1" pieces
- 1 large shallot, quartered
- 1 head of garlic, halved crosswise
- 6 sprigs flat-leaf parsley
- 1 tablespoon black peppercorns

MATZO BALLS
- 3 large eggs, beaten
- 3/4 cup matzo meal
- 1/4 cup schmaltz (chicken fat), melted
- 3 tablespoons club soda (my secret ingredient for fluffy, melt-in-you mouth balls)
- 1 1/4 teaspoon kosher salt

GARNISH
- 2 small carrots, peeled
- Pinch of kosher salt
- 2 tablespoons coarsely chopped fresh dill
- Coarsely ground fresh black pepper

PREPARATION

CHICKEN STOCK

- Bring all ingredients and 12 cups cold water to a boil in a very large (at least 12-qt.) stockpot. Reduce heat to medium-low and simmer until chicken breasts are cooked through and tender, about 20 minutes.

- Transfer breasts to a plate (remaining chicken parts are strictly for stock). Let breasts cool slightly, then remove meat and return bones to stock. Shred meat. Let cool, tightly wrap, and chill.

- Continue to simmer stock, skimming surface occasionally, until reduced by one-third, about 2 hours. Strain chicken stock through a fine-mesh sieve into a large saucepan (or airtight container, if not using right away); discard solids. You should have about 8 cups.

- **DON'T *VAIT!* DO AHEAD**: Stock can be made 2 days ahead. Let cool; cover and chill. Keep reserved chicken meat chilled.

MATZO BALL MIXTURE

- Mix beaten eggs, matzo meal, schmaltz, club soda, and salt in a medium bowl (mixture *vill* resemble *vet* sand; it *vill* firm up as it rests). Cover and chill at least 2 hours.

- **DO AHEAD**: Mixture can be made 1 day ahead. Keep chilled.

ASSEMBLY

- Bring chicken stock to a boil in a large saucepan. Add carrots; season *vith* salt.—Reduce heat and simmer until carrots are tender, 5–7 minutes. Remove from heat, add reserved breast meat, and cover. Set soup aside.

- *Meanvhile,* bring a large pot of *vell*-salted water to a boil. Scoop out 2-tablespoon-size portions matzo ball mixture and, using *vet* hands, gently roll into balls. (I LOVE ROLLING THE BALLS!)

- Add matzo balls to *vater* and reduce heat so *vater* is at a gentle simmer (too much bouncing around *vill* break them up). Cover pot and cook matzo balls until cooked through and starting to sink, 20–25 minutes. (DON'T LET THEM SINK ALL THE *VAY*. SINKERS ARE STINKERS!)

- **DO AHEAD**: Using a slotted spoon, transfer matzo balls to bowls. Ladle soup over, top *vith* dill, and season *vith* pepper. And enjoy!

ES GEZUNTERHEYT!

ABOUT THE AUTHOR

Nelle L'Amour is a *NEW YORK TIMES* and *USA TODAY* bestselling author who lives in Los Angeles with her Prince Charming-ish husband, twin teenage princesses, and a bevy of royal pain-in-the-butt pets. A former executive in the entertainment and toy industries with a prestigious Humanitus Award to her credit, she gave up playing with Barbies a long time ago but still enjoys playing with toys with her husband. While she writes in her PJs, she loves to get dressed up and pretend she's Hollywood royalty. She writes juicy stories with characters that will make you both laugh and cry and stay in your heart forever.

In addition to the *THAT MAN* series, she is the author of the bestselling erotic romance *Gloria's Secret* and its sequel, *Gloria's Revenge*, the *Seduced by the Park Avenue Billionaire* boxed set, and the highly rated Amazon bestseller, *Undying Love*.

Nelle loves to hear from her readers.

Sign up for her newsletter: http://eepurl.com/N3AXb

Email her at: nellelamour@gmail.com

Like her on Facebook: facebook.com/NelleLamourAuthor

And connect to her on Twitter: twitter.com/nellelamour

Printed in Great Britain
by Amazon.co.uk, Ltd.,
Marston Gate.